Tears in the dark

Shawn Freeman

Copyright © 2022 Shawn Freeman

ISBN:

DEDICATION

To my mom and dad, my first story tellers

And my grandmother Gloria, who still is my greatest story teller.

Contents

About this book.. *7*

Origins

Part one *9*

Scary Night in the New House

Part two

The quick sale

Part three.. *38*

The Scary Joke

Part four... *45*

The break down

Part five... *54*

The 911 call

Part six *64*

Psycho at large

Part seven *77*

Tears in the dark

The weeping child

ACKNOWLEDGMENTS

I would like to formally acknowledge all of the great artist who made the pictures in this book possible, the first shouting out to Mysticartdesign Mystic Art Design on pixabay and edit.org the designers of my book cover.

darksouls1 Enrique Meseguer from pixabay,chmphotography @chmphotography, Matthew T Rader @matthew_t_rader,ZoltanTasi @Zoltantasi,Kalhh and Kyle Johnson @kylejeffreys.All from the wonderful unsplash community.

Thank you all.

About this book

Origins

One night while sitting up late in my bed, working on my fifth story for this book well after midnight, the glare of the computer screen filled the surrounding dark r o o m , casting some light where I was sitting. I had no title yet for this book, and I was still working on my plan and organizing of the book, when all of a sudden I encountered a strange phenomenon.

The computer started to glitch. I assumed it was late and the computer was tired and needed a rest and to be honest so was I as well. Shutting down the computer and retiring to bed, I had a feeling of accomplishment because I had covered good grounds.

The next evening, up late again in my bed with ideas to start writing about. When I decided to fire up the computer, it refused to start up. All attempts to start the computer failed as I soon realized that the hard drive had crashed.

The unfortunate thing was, I was so busy with work that season, I didn't have time to back up my book. The only backing up done was the first two stories, unedited and parts unfinished. All my hard work was lost.

Well from that point, I took it as a sign that I should give up on this book. A few weeks after, I decided I was going to reprogram the computer but I should give it one more shot at starting up. To my shock and surprise, the computer started to load and started up as normal. A feeling of excitement came over me as I quickly searched for my book and found it all there, with only a few changes made unsaved. Well from that point I took that as a sign that I should finish this book and give it back to the world.

Remembering that faithful night sitting in the dark in sadness over the loss of my book, the title for the book was born.

Tears in the dark

It became a symbol for the bases of all the stories in this book about the unseen pain experienced in everyday life and the forgotten troubles we all face.

Each story is a testimony of experiences faced in those dark moments, when we feel pain that no one knows and cry tears no one sees.

This book is a reminder that not all stories have a happy ending, just like life but some actually do and can for those who fight for what they believe in and never stop trying. This book and its stories are a tribute to the fighters, regardless of a happy or sad end, it's a story worth talking about.

The supernatural encounters are a symbolic representation of actual events in our lives when we search for the answers to life's great questions to solve life's great problems. Regardless if supernatural or not, fighting and never giving up is what humanity is all about.

Tears in the dark is different because it takes fiction and turn it into reality, monsters do exist in the dark, supernatural or not and we do face unexplained challenges everyday but the zeal of the human soul pushes on for survival. This book is a shining example of every day encounters, some supernatural others aren't, parts could be fact or just fiction, each story shows the human nature in its true form.

It is with my best intentions and hope you enjoy reading this book and that you find your story as you remember your tears in the dark.

OH! By the way, I started backing up regularly ever since.

Part one

Scary Night in the New House

New houses are always a challenge to get used to, especially when it's creepy, and you happen to be living in it alone. They say your mind can play tricks on you, well so they say. Starting over life is already a great challenge, well that's the bases of this story, about Arthur and his new house.

5:45 p.m.- Art arrived when it's almost sun down to his new house, not new in the sense, because in Arts mind, old, leaky and possibly creaky, with lots of work to do on it. At the door, Arts mind went into flask back mode, when the door opened with a sound like the doors on castle Dracula. Art looks to his side, "what a Creepy, creaky door this one yeesh".

Unloading all the boxes in the house was a painful task for Art, with a killing back pain fetching five boxes, "right" he sighed, "I should have taken up on the gym sessions I paid for". Art thought. "Oh well" Art said to himself with a crooked smile of amusement as he continued unpacking.

7:15 p.m.-Art is sound asleep in his bed, tired from lifting those five boxes and unpacking, was suddenly awoken by a strange and eerie sound for outside. He slowly got up and went to the bedroom door, opening the door, he looked out in to the dark hallway, only to gasp at the dark silhouette figures of people standing in his living room looking straight at him. Art reached for the flash light he left next to the bedroom doorway, "thank god" he thought to himself he was too lazy to put it up, shining the flashlight into the dark hallway, to his surprise, no shadow people. "What the heck is going here?" Art cried. Looking at the corner of the living room window was a poster of his favorite band, which seem to cast a shadowy reflection again when the f l a s h l i g h t went off again. This he observed came from the streetlight coming through the window and reflecting through the poster held up against the window "I should have brought in those posters, but it looked so cool hanging up there". Art thought as he smiled with rolled up eyes.

6:55 a.m. - Art is up early and started off by finishing up on unpacking his stuff, while going thought some of his things, he discovered a mug that said number one mom, but Art wasn't a mother.
Flashing back as Art turns and looks to his left, Campus staff party, Arts last day at his old work place, he got so wasted he picked up his stuff from his desk and some from his colleague too. "Oh right" said Art with a devilish grin putting back the mug in the box.

8:45 a.m. - a bucket followed by a mop and Art behind are falling down the front stairs as; Art struggles to hold on to the rails. "What was that all about" shouted Art struggling to get up with a pain in his back.
Picking up the mop and bucket, he could clearly see the neighbors from a distance chuckling and a stray dog looking at him like I thought I had it bad.
He started remembering the agent telling him about the non-slip tiles on the stairways. "Yea right, non-slip my sore behind" he said to himself as he stomped up the stair way carrying the mop and bucket.

10:11 a.m. - Arts singing and dancing very freakishly and weird.
 11:38 a.m. - Arts having lunch.
12:51 p.m. – Arts dancing very freakishly and odd again.
1:56 p.m. - Arts asleep and snoring on the couch.
3:55 p.m. - Arts looking at a movie and crying, "Why am I crying? This movie isn't sad" Art said, followed by a loud outburst of crying.
5:21 p.m. - Arts locked outside the house. "Boy luckily I left the top floor window open" said Art panting for breath while crawling through the window.
7:41 p.m. - reaching into his fridge to pull out a bottle of orange juice, while drinking it down, a strange and eerie noise was heard from the basement, it sounded like crackling branches, Art cautiously moved to the wide open and dark basement doorway, as he looked down the dark staircase, the sounds got louder as he pushed his hand through the dark door way to flip on the basement light.
He glanced at the washing machines that was towards the right side corner of the basement where he could see a partly open window with breeze coming through. It was blowing up an open box of cracker jacks, he happened to have left when he was about to do the laundry but got distracted dancing and forgot to move it. "Well silly me" Art thought after the **flashback. Doing the super backup and move away gesture.** Art moved away from the basement door, flipped off the light switch and locked the door.

8:30 p.m. - Art in the washroom taking a burning release of urine with the door wide open, when all of a sudden he felt a cold breeze rushed passed him with great speed. "Hey what the?" said Art in shock as he turned around briskly, only to see nothing. Walking out the washroom door and looking around, he still saw nothing.

Art pulled up the top of his underpants "Yea that's right" Art said smiling while heading back to the washroom to continue his burning release of urine, when again, the rush of cold breeze swooshed passed the door.

Art turned around quickly and peered out the door. "Hey what's going on here?" Art asked confused, as he cautiously turned with hesitation to continue his burning need. Whoosh! Went the cold wind with speed passing the door yet again, this time Art took no chance; he scrambled for the washroom door and closed it shut.

8:38 PM- "interesting washroom break" said Art as he headed to switch off the living room lights, switching off the living room light came with a loud clap from the corner where the home entertainment set was, Arts pride and joy, especially dancing time. The strange sound was accompanied by, what sounded like soft laughter coming from the dark corner of the room. Art stared motionlessly into the now dark living room. 'Flip' went on the TV.

Art jumped back with astonishment. Moving slowly to the sofa where the remotes were, Art picked them up with a confused look on his face, "four remotes, how did I get to this?" Art said to himself. Art pressed the first remote, the TV switched off and the stereo switched on. He pressed the second remote, the stereo when off and the TV went back on. He then pressed the third remote, the TV and stereo when off then the Amplifier and sound board went on. At this time he was frustrated. He took all the remotes in hand and pressed them together with a wild and crazy grin. Sparks and flashes of light went, as the power supply got blown up with loud electric sparks. **Doing the super backup and move away gesture, Art backed away** but while turning briskly in the dark room, he bumped into something standing behind him. **"AAAAAAHHHH what the…."** The remotes in his hands flung in the air as Art struggled. Flipping back on the living room lights, he saw lying on the floor, a large coat rack with coats.

"Since when did I have a coat rack, and where did this hat come from?" shouted Art.

Art thought as he **flashes back while turning to his left,** dancing freakishly with a hat on his head and the coat rack in his hands as a guitar in living room hallway. "Oooh right" said Art smiling.

9:01 p.m. - its bath and brush teeth time for Art. In front of the mirror in the bathroom, he gasped at the reflection of shoes very visible at the bottom of the drawn shower curtains, motionless was the shoes, so was Art, as he finally got some sense bravery and reached to the side of the bathroom sink to pick up a weapon. Looking at the toilet brush in his hand, Art knows that this wasn't right, quickly putting it down and picking up a long Swiffer broom clutched firmly in his hand. Art swung wildly at the shower curtains, knocking over the bathroom cabinet and the shower curtains in the process, the sound of smashing glass was heard too as the shower curtains iron r o d broke off and flew out hitting the bathroom window. In the bathtub was a pair of sneakers. "Now how did sneakers get in here?" Art shouted loudly with frustration while looking down at the pair of shoes. Art thought as he **flashes back while turning to his left,** dancing freakishly with the shoes on his feet in the bathtub. "Ooh right". Art said to himself while slapping his forehead.

10:10 p.m. - "wow! What a day" said Art as he dried off his skin with the towel and prepared for bed. Laughing to himself "I really need to take it easy" he thought. "The only weird and strange thing in this house is surprisingly me". He thought. "Oh well" Art shrugged his shoulders and switched off his bedroom lights to make his way off to bed.

While lying in bed, he was about to fall off to sleep, WAIT! Dragging his hand to his side without turning around, he could feel the physical shape and figure of someone lying in his bed next to him. The sheet covering over the figure from head to toe, he was sacred to turn around as he felt a slight jerk in his back. Someone was definitely lying next to him….

His eyes opened wide as he started into the darkness.

oooOH Shhhhhh!

Part two

The quick sale

In the world of fast business, the quick sale is the moneymaker, with big profits and high risk, some will do anything for a quick sale to make that quick buck. This is the bases of this story, about a young man who's good at selling anything to anyone, a man who will sell anything to make the big score, well just about anything.......

Jose Kemp, the new guy in a thriving business and already a BMW parked outside his house, as if the swimming pool constructing in the backyard wasn't enough, his neighbors heard him boasting about a second wing to be constructed on his already large condo. Kemp was a salesman of the century, even sold someone's discarded junk back to them for a profit. Two weeks at William Park's and Associates Insurance Firm, and he's already got it made. Probably will make partner soon with a well struck record sale streak of 12 policies sold every week, some only get one a week, if they are lucky. The thought that someone so new to the company could be well accomplished was enough to make a few jealous, especially the senior's staff.
Jose greeted everyone pleasantly when he came in, another sales tactic well deployed, he could really sell himself as well, and everyone except one bought the sales pitch. Luther, sales rep of five years and once the top man in the company who held out for the sales manager position until Jose showed up and took it clean from under his wings. This left a bitter taste in one's mouth as Luther plain out didn't like Jose for this and other reasons.
One Christmas season, Luther collected holiday greeting cards to give out to all staff and intentionally discarded Jose's card in the bin. The rivalry between them one time almost got out of hand when Jose as his boss asked him to pick up on the sales as he was the only one in the department behind.

Luther with both fist punched on the table leaned over in front of Jose's face then asked him "if there would be anything else?". Jose calmly turned away from him and said "no that will be all".
Jose's attitude towards work and everything else made him the success he was, a person who everyone spoke well of and some admired.
Change was in the atmosphere as Mr. Taylor his boss and company CEO, was busy in meetings daily discussing something very important with the company's top executives. This had most staff members curious about what was going on and when the big news would be discussed with them.
That day finally came when a general staff meeting was called in the common staff room. Mr. Taylor was very excited and wasted no time to deliver his speech, which was unusual and a surprise for most since he was the type of guy that would go around in a never finishing circle before he actually said what he needed to say. Most staff members already prepared for this, calls to family members for late picks to

13

On both sides of the mansion was well furnished with the finest vintage furniture with a large hallway space standing between them.

To the far right of the mansion he noticed an indoor swimming pool and what seemed to be a beautiful and stunning young woman in a bikini swimming in it, as she came out of the pool, Jose quickly turned away his face embarrassed especially at the thought that she may have noticed him looking.

"Hi don't be shy" she said with a pretty smile as she walked up to him.

This caused Jose to blush as he turned around and smiled, he was hoping she didn't notice the change in his face color. She was drying off her hair with a towel as she came up close to Jose and extended out her hand in a gesture for a handshake.

"You must be him, huh?" She said looking at Jose from head to toe. This made him a little more uncomfortable since it seems like she was checking him out. Jose actually wasn't a bad looking guy either, with a well fit body, in very good health, top with a college degree. He wasn't too shabby.

"I beg your pardon madam?" Jose asked

"The insurance guy" she said with a giggle.

"Oh yes yes" Jose replied now with a flushed look of embarrassment.

Before she could introduce herself and say anything else, the butler returned. He looked at her with a serious face and said "Madam the masseuse just arrived and is waiting in the massage room".

"Ok great" she replied. She turned to Jose and said "I guess I'll be seeing you around" with another one of those cute smiles that made Jose blush as he replied with a sharp "yes" in a low tone.

Just as she walked off, the phone rang. It was an old fashion custom type phone used back in the 30s or 40s and was conveniently placed not too far from the front door. The butler walked over to where it was to answer it, Jose could hear him saying yes sir, right away sir.

"The master will see you now; the meeting however will have to be taken to his bedroom instead"

Jose nodded in reply as he started to prepare his mind for the challenge he was about to face in a few minutes.

Already a nervous encounter with what may have been his daughter or granddaughter; he knew that a steady head was needed this time with no time for distractions.

Jose straightened up his tie and quickly brushed down his suit as he walked up the staircase with his briefcase in hand.

What Jose saw when he entered the bedroom sent shock waves straight through his spine.

The bedroom was very large and well decorated with the finest bedroom furnishing, it also had all sorts of state of the art technological equipment, from large monitors to advanced dialysis machines and respiration equipment with oxygen tanks all surrounding a king-sized bed, lying on the bed was Dr. Don Lichtenstein.

This caught Jose off guard since none of his research showed the eighty one-year-old successful doctor and businessman as being that sick. With doctors and nurses attending to his every need, there were servants moving around and picking up and packing things, it looked to Jose like this was a fancy private hospital of some sort and a very high-tech one at best.

"Don't be nervous" said Don Lichtenstein pulling down a respirator mask with a smile. "These doctors have given it there best and having a little company today won't kill me" he chuckled in his throat while coughing slightly.

16

From research there was less about the doctor, he didn't take many pictures of himself or was very social.

"I know you're from the insurance company and my sources told me that you're very good at what you do" he said while giving Jose a smile of amusement.

Jose was again overwhelmed as the thought of a client actually researching him was a game changer, however the game face was on and Jose was about to give it his best shot.

"Yes Good day sir, I have picked out an excellent policy for you that I know you would like" before Jose could go on, he was interrupted by Don Lichtenstein who waved to his butler in a calling fashion, he then came and leaned over the bed as Don Lichtenstein whispered something in his ear. Soon after, the butler announced that all persons in the room were to leave immediately.

This caused everyone to leave what they were doing and exited the door, only the Butler stayed; he walked over to the far end of the bedroom window and stood at attention.

There was a large 70-inch television in the corner of the room set on the news channel; Jose could hear the news anchor reading out the headlines.

"Today, tragedy struck Gem Haven as the faceless killer struck again" as the news anchor when on "A group of college students also in Gem Haven….." Don Lichtenstein signaled to the butler to switch off the television, which he did immediately in the middle of the announcement.

"Mr. Jose I'll be direct with you and spare you the time, the same time I know I don't have". "I know everything about these policies because I wrote what you studied" he said this with a sharp look, one that froze Jose into a block of ice. He was speechless.

"However I have an offer for you instead, if you want the sale all you have to do is agree" Dr. Don Lichtenstein gave him another sharp look that now confused him.

"I beg your pardon sir". "Look, as a man ages leaving his loved ones behind as well as all he had accomplished is the one thing he thinks about, thus the reason why these policies exist, simply because people think about death and family" he turned to the butler standing at the window and signaled him again.

The butler understood the gesture and briskly walked over to the bed and leaned over. As the doctor whispered in the butlers ears they both turned and looked at Jose. After the conversion was over, the butler asked for an excuse and left. Before the butler closed the door, he gave Jose a cold stare with an unusual grin. This made him very nervous now.

"My wife, God bless her, encouraged me to take out a new lease on life, as a matter and fact she's the one reason I keep thinking about life" he said while chuckling and choking at the same time. "I guess you met already, in the hallway downstairs" he said while looking at Jose with a wide smile followed by a wink.

Far from his thoughts Jose had thought it was his daughter or granddaughter, no wonder he thought so much about life.

"Well life and death has its meaning but for me life without death sounds rather spectacular" he said with a happy grin on his face.

"I'm sorry sir but why did you ask me to come here" Jose asked puzzled now. The butler had entered the room again and was standing next to the window as usual.

"Life Mr. Kemp, that's why you're here and why I need you" he said while rising up in a sitting position.

The butler rushed over to assist him, but he just waved him away. "You're a man that's good with deals and I want to make you deal of a lifetime, actually it's all about life" he said while chuckling.
"I'm afraid I don't understand sir" Jose said confused.

"The deal is simple Mr. Kemp so pay attention". He waved to the butler to come over and pointed to a draw; the butler opens the draw and took out a large brown cover book that looked ancient with strange symbols and writings. "I know what you're thinking and your right, this book is as old as time but has proven its worth" "how so sir" asked Jose curious.
"That you will find out soon enough my boy" he replied with a grin.
Doctor Don Lichtenstein opened the book and started searching through pages; his eyes were wide with anticipation as he landed on a page that had what appeared to be a drawing of a large box with gears around it. He encouraged Jose to listen carefully as he explained and assured him that his time would not be wasted as he already spoke to his employer requesting the over time. He seemed to be a very powerful person from what Jose could see, he had a manner of authority of always being sure of everything.

The levels of control he had and personal under his command showed this and the fact that one simple call awarded him over time from the company, something that requires great effort to request from Mr. Taylor, only made Jose more interested to see how this meeting will turn out. After all he was promised that it would be worth his time and this person doesn't seem to joke around when it comes to time or business.
Jose could see him struggling to read the pages as he adjusted his reading glasses, the pages in the book were in some sort of foreign language that looked ancient.
"Ah the Tithonus machine, the giver of life and restorer of youth" he said with a big smile. "Let me tell you the whole story".

The Tithonus, the immortal who forgot to ask for youth.

As he began to tell the story, Jose listened attentively, for Jose this was a new experience. Never before have a customer been able to captivate his attention. He was like a school boy sitting in classroom listening to his teacher teaching. The butler brought a chair for him to sit, and he quickly took a seat.
This story starts in a small village in Italy, in a humble home of farmers, who had one son they loved very much, and he loved back equally.
As faith would have it they were taken away by a tragic accident on their way to the marketplace to sell their goods. This tore the young man apart as he was broken up with grief and plunged into depression, so much that he questioned life and death itself and wasn't satisfied with the answers he got. In his grief, he was determined to solve life's great mystery.

He spent most of his time searching through the university's library, relying on the fact that he was a scientific genius in natural science at the university; the professors didn't mind it at all helping him with his questions which in most cases ended up nowhere. Desperate and running out of answers, the young man felt that his search for the answers he was looking for would never be answered, until one day a visiting professor from a foreign country caught his attention, as this man was not only talented in science but also folklore and the study of archaeology. What caught the young man's attention was the fact that they shared the same common interest in unlocking the mysteries of death.

An academic bond was quickly formed when the dean of the natural sciences department requested that the young man work alongside him as his apprentice. The two worked together very well, two geniuses trying to solve one problem.

Until one day the solution came to them, while researching, they found records from Greece, this told a story about a prince of Troy called Tithonus who fell in love with the goddess of Dawn, Eos, being a mortal man it was difficult to have a normal life with an immortal Goddess.

Eos eventually took Tithonus as her husband and asked Zeus to grant him immortality as her wedding gift.

Zeus agreed and granted Tithonus immortality, and they lived together very happy, however the gift was incomplete since she forgot to ask for forever youth and Tithonus aged, one day Tithonus grew sad and troubled living an immortal life as an old man, while his family, friends and subjects died. This made him so depressed that he no longer lived happy with his wife. This upset Eos very much, Eos while looking at a once the handsomest man in all Greece now old, decided to fix the issue.

Eos called a meeting with the God of knowledge and Olympian master builders. Together they would formulate a solution to the problem they faced.

They would create a machine that would be able to reverse aging and restore youth. They called this machine the Tithonus machine. The principle operation was simple, once inside, he would repeat words inscribed inside the great machine that confirmed his request and the process could begin. As the story ended, both the young man and his new partner looked at each other and smiled. They would spend weeks on ends researching the details about this machine, until finally they were ready to perform a bold experiment that combined the skills of science and the assistance of dark magic. The machine was finally finished and ready for testing.

Records showed success of this machine however not much was described after its completion or any confirmation it actually works. It was declared an old wives tale.

As the story ended, Jose was shocked with astonishment and sat speechless. Dr. Don Lichtenstein closed the book and took off his glasses. "Well there you go" he said with a big smile. "I promised a good story".

"You certainly did sir" smiled Jose.

"Well after I came across this book many decades ago, I only kept thinking about Tithonus machine" he said as he handed the book to his butler. "The good news is after many years of research and millions of dollars invested my dear boy, I've actually built this machine" he looked at Jose delighted.

Jose laughed as he said this and thought to himself, what a senile old man. The most absurd but good story, yet still just a story to Jose.

He could see form the expression on his face that his laughter seemed to have offended the doctor, after which Jose stopped laughing and quickly adopted a serious look on his face.

"I see you find my story very funny my boy, but I can assure you it's very much real" after saying this he signaled for his butler to bring a document that was resting on the opposite side of the bed on a table that was full of medications resting on it. As the butler handed him the papers, he called Jose to come closer to the bedside.

As Jose came and stood next to the bed, he could clearly see the document was a William Park's and Associates Insurance Firm policy papers. Shocked that he already was in possession of this document; cast some questions in Jose's mind as to what's really going on.

"Here is the answer to all your problems and mine" he said lifting the papers up in front of Jose. "I will sign this document that will land your company in a very well established position and you my boy will be the hero of the hour but only under one condition" he said this with a crooked grin.

"What would that be" Jose asked curiously.

"A simple exchange of your SOUL" he said this sharply as he stared at Jose.

Once again Jose was thinking about his craziness and how much he seemed to believe in it.

This didn't surprise Jose at all really, as this was the second time in his career he had to deal with a delusional old man who had a large amount of cash lying around and could have afforded to be crazy.

This last guy believed that if he was given a policy which was approved the same day on Friday the 13th, he would be transformed into a supernatural being and escapes death.

For Jose this was only just quick paper work and a quick sale, same thing he was staring at right now.

Jose was never a religious person, especially after losing his parents at an early age and having to fend for himself, the only religion he actually believed in was the sale.

He felt somehow connected to the story; he was sure the doctor even researched his life history and quickly tied this into his favorite bedtime story book. Perfect and clear to Jose this guy was crazy and crazy rich too.

"So you're saying all I have to do is say yes, and the agreement will be signed" Jose asked.

"Very much so my boy" he said with a satisfied smile. "Only one more thing to add to that" he said. "And what's that?" asked Jose. "The machine needs the actual same ritual of you reciting just a few words" he said.

Now Jose was sure he was crazy and would do anything just to amuse himself. Jose agreed but hesitantly as this seemed ethically wrong on certain grounds, however entertaining clients is nothing new to him. He once dressed up as circus clown to win the affection of a client's kids. However, the case, something about this client seemed very unusual, and he couldn't help having the feeling something was wrong.

The Tithonus machine
the restorer of life an youth

The butler picked up the bedroom phone and spoke very quietly, after he was finished, he hung up the phone, turned to the doctor and nodded.

"Well Mr. Jose shall we?" He asked. Right after he finished his question, three persons knocked an entered the room dressed in lab coats. They had very serious expressions on their faces and said nothing as they entered the room. One of scientist asked "Are we ready". The butler looked at the doctor and both nodded.

He then turned to the other two scientists, one a female of Asian descent and the male of Caucasian descent and nodded, they both then nodded in response and headed off to a corner of the room that had a plain wall, strangely this side of the room had no pictures on the wall, and it was just plain.

The head scientist walked up to join them, as he stood in front the wall with the others; he pulled out what appeared to be an electronic key card. It had strange writings that looked like an ancient language. He recognized the same language in the book the doctor was reading from.

He held it up in front of a light switch, the light switch started to glow red then a blue laser light scanner started scanning the ID key card, it then started to blink as though it was some high-tech wireless security scanner lock. After which there was a noise coming from behind the wall, then all four corners of the wall pushed in, florescent lights came on from behind the wall reveling a secret room.

Jose looked on in astonishment, never before in his life did he ever see anything like this before. He stood motionless as he watched the scientist enter the secret room from behind the wall.

While all this was going on a maid had entered the room with a wheelchair and was assisting the butler to put the doctor in.

"Well off we go" the doctor said cheerfully as he was being pushed in the wheelchair by his butler. Jose followed slowly behind still amazed, as he approached the entrance he could feel a cold breeze coming from inside, one that was generated by a very cool air conditioner.

21

As Jose stepped inside, he could see very high-tech computer equipment, data monitors with large displays screens and a large mainframe data logger.

At the center of the secret room a strange machine caught Jose's eyes. A large complex machine of glass and gears, it had the same strange ancient writing he kept seeing often, it was written all over the glass box, wires and tubes were connected to it hooked up to a large data logger. The machine gears varied in style and shapes and somewhere gold and silver.

As the scientist opened the doors of the machine, the top and bottom of the machine activated an ultra-bright white light that was so bright Jose had to cover his eyes.

He could hear the scientist discussing something about the machine as they stood in front of a large computer monitor.

At this point, Jose was confused as to what was really going on and what he really agreed to do, but his logical mind could only tell him this was nothing but an old man's craziness.

The head scientist came over to them and said that the machine was ready when they are. He then turned to Jose and started to explain what was going on.

He told him that the machine is controlled by them on the outside, all he had to do was enter the machine and once the doors are closed, read the words inscribed on a piece of paper he handed to him, it was in the same strange ancient language. The head scientist interpreted the words and asked him to repeat it to make sure he remembers the words, it sounded like some form of ancient Greek, but it wasn't difficult to remember as Jose had a very good memory and the words were very short, no more than a sentence.

"You really went all the way out for this fantasy of yours doc" Jose said laughing.

"You can say that" said the doctor with a chuckle. "Ok how do you play this game" Jose asked.

"Simple, all you do is enter the chamber and repeat the words when the door closes and when the lights go out the magic begins" the doctor chuckled at the phrase.

This was all silly Jose thought, playing this game just to make a sale but a big sale he thought and one that comes with a huge promotion. So for Jose this game was worth the playing.

"Ok well let's get on with it, so I can get going" Jose said impatiently.

At this time Jose was bored by of all the theatrics as impressive as it was, this sort of games can go sour after a while.

His thoughts of how far one person have gone to put together the most unusual belief, amazed Jose. To him all of this looked like a bunch of baloney anyway.

He noticed a bunch of abnormalities with the whole thing.

First, the computers data loggers seemed to be running some old data with really fancy animations, something a computer graphic designer could do in a heartbeat, he remembered the companies IT guys and how good they are at software engineering and this guy looks like he could have hired the best to make his fantasy look superb.

Secondly all the jumbo gears seemed to be self-operational as they were not connected to an electronic mechanism or anything, how are the gears going to move, certainly not by them self, he chuckled at the thought.

"Right this way" said one of the scientists.

As Jose followed, he could see as he looked back for a brief moment that a lot of discussion was going on and what appeared to be a brief show of anger from the doctor at one of the scientist. Very unusual behavior he thought to himself, but the cold feeling still lingered in his mind that all this somehow didn't seem right.

Entering the chamber, Jose noticed the machine of glass and gears seem to work well together as he looked down he could see another set of gears on the floor of the machine and some on top, they all started turning as he entered the machine.

The words on the glass glowed as though it was painted with neon glow paint and a strange hissing sound of gas entered the chamber from a hose connection to a tank from the outside the machine.

At this point Jose was getting a bit worried as it started to dawn on him this may not be a game at all, however a sight of comfort came as he saw one of the scientist at the back of the machine turning a leaver handle that seemed to be turning the gears he saw moving at the bottom and top of the machine.

Cheap bastard couldn't even buy an automatic working machine. Jose thought as he smiled at the thought that he may be looking at some of his servants dressed up as scientists and another joke came to mind, maybe the other scientist will turn a leaver somewhere to work the rest of the gears, Jose chuckled to himself.

"All set sir" said one of the scientists looking at the computer monitor. "The engine is priming, and the crystal has almost reached its energy level" he smiled as he looked at the doctor. "Good all good my darlings" said the doctor with a happy expression on his face. "Remember sir you enter before the end" winked the scientist.

"Yes, yes I remember" smiled the doctor as he turned to look at Jose. "Thank you my dear friend, you have given me something words can't explain, and I will give it all back".

At this time Jose was quiet and still as calm waters on a lake, waiting for what comes next. He could hear lots of sounds now in the machine and more of the words started to glow, it seemed to be all happening as a large crystal started to glow; light beams came out of it as it got brighter.

This was the biggest crystal Jose ever saw but thought to himself that this could be responsible for the words glowing because he heard that some crystals can produce UV light that could cause objects to become energized and glow.

"Remember as the lights go out in the machine, read the words out loud and that's it, you're done" said one of the scientist. Jose nodded and showed thumbs up as the scientist turned and walked over to the control station, he started entering typing something on the computer keyboard and signaled the other scientist from the other end of the control station.

Jose could see the machine doors starting to close, it began vibrating slightly. As the door closed the gears at the bottom and top of the machine started to spin faster and faster, looking back Jose could see that there was no one turning nothing and the machine was now doing this by itself. The gears on the side of the machine started turning as well and soon picked up with speed.

He could feel a big gust of wind blowing in the chamber and just in time as well, the machine seemed to be airtight and it was getting harder to breathe. This scared Jose a bit, but he remained calm and hope in his mind for this to be over soon, so he could leave this silliness behind.

Suddenly, all the words on the glass started to glow bright as the crystal also produced more and more beams of light rays.

The top and bottom lights on the machine got very bright at this time, Jose covered his eyes as the light was blinding, the machine started to vibrate more violently as the gears started to spin faster, when Jose squinted his eyes, he could see it spinning as fast as a jet turbine. At this time, his mind was racing as to what's really going on here. Jose's mind started racing as his entire life started flashing uncontrollably before him; his whole childhood appeared in front of him from his painful memory he felt being bullied in school to his graduation from high school, he even saw his first love and the heartache he felt when they parted.

How he played brave as, they said their goodbyes but silently cried every day since and his university graduation all the success that day celebrated but looked around at the other students with their families and friends as he stood alone holding his award. Tears ran from his face as he fell to the floor sobbing uncontrollably. The light in the chamber now intensified when suddenly everything when pitch black and the machine stop vibrating, Jose could hear the gears slowing down and coming to a stop.

Jose wiped the tears from his eyes and stood up in the dark chamber, he then started reciting the words he had to say. As soon as he finished the last word he could hear the doors of the machine opening and the top and bottom lights came on first with a soft dim glow and brightened up. It was over.

Jose walked out the machine feeling no way different except emotionally distressed at the flashback of memories he experienced in the chamber. It was strange how it actually happened, playing like a video recording in sequence with precise order of events.

He didn't even realize that so much time had gone by as the digital wall clock at the far corner of the secret room read 7:35pm from Jose's count he was in the machine for at least three hours, yet it only felt like ten minutes. At this stage Jose was confused, emotionally distressed and late; he's not a night owl and late nights out is not his thing.

The other feeling of hunger came as he missed dinner, he was very much fine overall and very anxious to leave and go home, as it is, he played along and the deal was done, the quickest sale for him actually too longer than he thought and only tomorrow will tell of its rewards.

"Well that wasn't so bad wasn't it?" asked the doctor. Jose replied with a soft "no", while looking back at the machine again, the machine stood still and calm as though nothing happened, everything seemed like a just a dream.

"I bet you must be hungry?" asked the doctor. Jose replied once again softly "yes".

"Well why not stay for dinner, I'd love it if you stay" the doctor said with a delighted look on his face.

Jose declined the offer and indicated to the doctor that he really had to get going, Jose couldn't help but noticing a strange look in the doctor's eyes as he often stared at him with an unusual look.

Jose was gathered all of his things and was preparing to leave, when he was stopped at the door by one of the doctor's servants. It was the maid that was helping the butler earlier. She told Jose she needed to talk to him but by the stairway as cameras were watching them. When the butler came out to ask if everything was alright, she quickly turned to the butler before Jose could say anything and answered "Yes I was helping Mr. Kemp with his things". The butler held out the signed contracts Jose forgot to collect, He said thank you as he collected the documents, Jose couldn't help noticing the scared and nervous look on the maid's face as the butler turned and looked at her, one quick glance at Jose, and he walked away.

At the end of the stairway, the maid met him, grabbing his hand firmly as if to pull him over the rails, Jose took hold of the rails with his right hand while clutching his briefcase with the left. "The cameras aren't here, so we are safe" she said with a nervous expression on her face.

"You have to undo what you did son" she said, Jose looked at her with a loss for words, but before he could say anything she began talking again. "You have until he dies, everything starts after that, everything" she repeated as her voice raised to a high pitch stressing the word everything, she then continued, "then three days after, after which......" she was then suddenly interrupted by the butler who standing behind her, he said with a sharp raised voice "Miss Larson you're needed in the master's kitchen". She froze with a look of terror.

She turned once more to look at Jose and walked off very briskly. Jose couldn't help noticing how scared she looked when the butler showed up and the look of sadness as she walked away.

"You have to excuse some of our staff sir, they have been with us so long, keeping them on after they encounter emotional problems is the least we could do" he said with a confident British accent as he made a gesture showing Jose to the door.

Jose couldn't get out of his mind as he walked to his car what the maid told him and the way she was so scared when she saw the butler. What really did he get himself in this time? The drive home felt long as he kept going over and over in his mind what the maid tried to tell him. What did she mean?

Jose had a restless night, trying to sleep was difficult, his dreams were a mix of memories with night terrors, it kept him awake most of the night. He kept dreaming of nightmarish creatures coming out of the machine and dragging him inside. He got up and sat in his bed with his hands covering his face, beads of perspiration running down his body. For once in his life he was really felt confused and a little scared.

The death of Doctor Don Lichtenstein

The next day at work, it was excitement as Jose walked in the hero of the hour, he was rushed first by his staff then some others staff from the various departments who came up to him and said "we all know that could do it".

Luther sat at his desk pretending to be busy but never got up to say anything to him. Before Jose could go to his office, Mr. Taylor's secretary came up to his and said "the boss would like to see you now". Looking at his office door Jose could see his name tag on it was gone.

Mr. Taylor was in good spirits and very cheerful as he entered. "Sit down my son, sit down". He said cheerfully. Jose could see bottles of wine in a box across the office as a celebration was somehow in order, he found it even strange as this was something even he didn't encourage at work, drinking.

"You don't know how much I and the staff are grateful to you for this deal" Mr. Taylor said as he sat back in his chair with a smile.

"Just doing my job sir" Jose said with an uneasy smile. "This was more than just a job, this is a life changer for this business from now on and especially for you" Mr. Taylor said as he got up and walked over to the office window opposite his chair, it was a very large window facing the city, it allowed plenty of light to shine in the office, but today it was shining brightly on Taylor.

It was to note that William Park's and Associates Insurance Firm was one of the well established firms in the country as well as building size, Taylor's office alone showed its magnitude in size as self-contained office with very large windows overlooking the city. Taylor stared out the window for some time in silence before he begins taking again. "This company was established by William Taylor, my father and his friends during economic hardship in this city, from jobs to financial bailouts to insurance supports for the small man and his family, my father grew this business and up until yesterday Jose my friend we were about to go under in financial ruin".

This came as a shock to Jose as he always thought the business did well in terms of sales but then accounting logistics wasn't his thing. "As now chairman of this company's board, I take special interest in its growth and success as a family business and whatever measures or steps have to be taken to save it, I'll do it". He said these words while still looking out the window.

"One day you will understand" he turned around and stared at Jose with a serious but blank and cold expression.

Jose stood and listened as it came to him more clearly now that this was a career move for Taylor as well moving up to the majority shareholder in his father's company, he was the legacy of a great family business however with not many shares as thought.

As he could hear laughter from outside the office, Taylor spoke before he could say anything. "And yes you're the hero of the hour, everyone was given the day off with a long overdue raise" he smiled widely as Jose said "well for that I'm glad". "But before I let you go" Taylor called in his secretary and ordered for the contract file, she brought it in immediately turned and looked at Jose with a smile and exited the office.

Taylor now back sitting in his chair with the file open said "As agreed the partner position and new office that comes with it" he smiled as he handed Jose the documents and said "you saved this company and me son".

Jose took the documents and started to read for no more than a few seconds when he was interrupted by Taylor, ordering him to sign, as everything he could explain, but Jose asked politely just to have a read through for formality's sake. Taylor however insisted that he just make haste and sign as he had a celebration to start before he sent everyone home, and he could read through it later when he gets his personal copy.

Jose agreed, not wanting to keep everyone back and signed, it still didn't matter to him anyhow since he was going to accept the promotion anyway, and reading through the contract wasn't much of a big deal.

The office get together was the best he saw in a long time, even Luther was there and enjoyed himself as Jose noticed he raised a glass to him and drank with a smile. Jose was now after the whole ordeal relaxed and happy.

A few weeks had passed as Jose took up the new position and started to question certain small things, such as who was the new CEO as Taylor's duties now has changed to running the board as chairman and documents of great importance to the company was often left undone.

Taylor would often dismiss his queries as one time a document came from the board was delivered for him to sign off. A junior partner doesn't have the power or authority to sign off board approval documents and for Jose this was getting too strange, to also add to the strange upgrades in the job, a company car, convertible to be exact and a salary that certainly wasn't one fitting a junior partner. It was five times larger than what was the norm for the position. However, the suspicion Jose wasn't one to complain, after all Mr. Taylor did said he saved the company, and he was very grateful for what he had done.

One day while looking at the news from his office, Jose was shocked at the headlines, as it read out that the famous contributor to the world science and medicine, Doctor Perry Tripper has passed away.

This shocked Jose right out his seat, he rose knocking over his cup of coffee on the table causing a great mess as it spilled all over the documents he was reviewing, his mind now crowded with questions, why was he called Don Lichtenstein and his name was Perry Tripper?

Then Jose got a smart idea that maybe he got a name change, people often change their name and that's no big deal.

Still strange as it was, could explain why from his research, he saw a profile for a different person.

The news continued to speak about his contributions to the medical field and his charitable contributions, but all Jose's mind again wondered off to was what the maid had said to him a few weeks ago. Now more than ever Jose's relaxed state of began started to change as a sharp pain struck him in his chest, it was so painful that he fell to the ground, his eyes started blurring out as he struggled to get up to call out for help, but he couldn't. The pain was so much Jose passed out for some time on the floor as he came too and got up off the floor, he noticed three hours had gone by. What had happened to him made him really worried him as he tried to pack up his things to go home. He suddenly heard a whisper calling his name from outside the office, it sounded faint but loud enough for him to hear.

As he opened the door and looked out the office he could see it was dark and everyone had gone home. Just a few office lights and computers left on, he couldn't see anything, as he picked up his bag to walk out a sudden gust of wind blew into the office causing all the open office doors to slam shut.

He could once again hear a faint whisper calling his name in the still quietness of the office, Joooooossseee this caused him to get a little nervous as he looked around and saw no one. Suddenly as he turned to walk down the stairs, a dark shadowy figure stood in the hallway leading to the stairs, it had the appearance of a man in a wheelchair, and he could hear finger nails tapping on the chair's steel handle which then turned to the sound of loud scratching as the nails dragged along the chair handle. He couldn't make out a face, but something told him this strange figure before him was the doctor, but that couldn't be as he was dead.

The wheelchair slowly started moving towards him as he tried to back up and move away, the wheel chair started to move faster down the hall as Jose keep backing up the faster the wheelchair kept moving towards him, he could hear an evil chuckle coming from the person in the wheelchair, as Jose turned to run he bumped into something standing behind him that grabbed him by both arms.

It was his boss Mr. Taylor, "Hey Jose is everything ok it looks like you've seen a ghost?" Mr. Taylor laughed. Jose turned around briskly but the shadowy figure was gone. He stood looking into the dark hallway speechless, then turned to Taylor and said "I'm fine" with a nervous look on his face. "I know the feeling trust me, working this late can really take a tow on you, go home and get some rest" he tapped him on the shoulder and walked off. It came to Jose a mystery why Taylor was working that late in the office when everyone was gone but he never asked and the strange experience he just encountered caused him to forget about Taylor's late working and more about what happened as he suddenly now grew more worried and concern, one thing now crossed his mind and that was to go back the mansion to talk to the maid again.

Day one

Arriving at the mansion it was evident that preparations for the funeral was on the way, as Jose looked around, he didn't see the maid but sighted Doctor Don Lichtenstein's wife, who seemed not broken up or sad at all, for that fact her normal massage appointment was in order as she didn't have the time to meet anyone. Jose was greeted by the butler who expressed how surprised he was at seeing him.

Jose returned the pleasant greeting and gave his condolences and asked that his regrets be passed on the doctor's wife, the butler said "very well sir". Jose then asked if he could speak with the maid he had spoken to on his last visit.
Ms. Larson was the name given by the butler; however he was told that Ms. Larson was on extended vacation.

Jose tried to ask if he could get a contact number or address for her, but the butler told him that employee's information is confidential, Jose tried to interject by saying she tried to have a conversation with him and wouldn't mind him trying to contact her, but before he could continue his argument the butler cut him off by saying, how busy it is around the mansion with all the preparations for the wake and funeral and he had to take his leave and return. As he turned and walked away, he said something that c a u s e d Jose to raise his brows in suspicion, he said "congratulations on your promotion master".
On his way back to the office, he couldn't help the overwhelming feeling that something was terribly wrong and the more he thought about it the more he started to think about the Tithonus machine and the story he was told, and maybe it wasn't a story at all, as impossible as it sounds he knew that he needed to get answers.

At the office Jose was at his old office still vacant as a replacement wasn't selected yet, but he somehow felt more comfortable especially in times of troubles being in it. Sitting at his old computer and desk brought back memories of his first week at the company and how every day since the old computer help him out of some really serious jams. Searching for the machine online and even with some companies independent research teams the company used to research information and clients proved futile, he was about to give up in despair when he heard a voice behind him and one he didn't expect to hear either.
"Seems like you need some help there?" ask Luther. As Jose turned around he could see Luther standing behind him with a curious look on his face. "As a matter and fact I think I do" replied Jose with a look of frustration. "Well from what I saw you

certainly do pal" Luther said as he moved closer to him with both his hands in his pocket. "My apologies but I couldn't help overlooking your research into the occult and folklore".

At this point Jose was in shock and surprise to see that Luther actually was talking to him and despite all that was going on in his life nothing could have been stranger than that.

Jose was desperate and frustrated to think about friend and foe and opened up to talking to Luther about all that was happening and what he suspected was going on. Luther took a seat in the chair next to him and listened attentively as Jose explained, after the explanations were finished, Luther's eyes got wider with fascination after hearing the story. He told Jose that his family were decedents of a proud Amerindian tribe that believed in mystical spirits and folklore and, he went on to also reveal that he was sort of a hobbyist paranormal investigator.

This was very good news to Jose, especially when he offered to take up his case, he couldn't help thinking what an interesting turn of events he was experiencing, first a body snatching soul machine, an unusual promotion and an enemy now a friend.

Luther told him that he never really hated him at all even though he did get a bit jealous, it was a miscommunication as he thought he hated him, he recalled when he first got stepped up in the department, his first order of business was to call all the poor performing employees, and he was first on the list.

They both laughed it off as Jose told him he honestly just wanted to talk to him first because he knew that he was the best and only tied to push him to get back there.

"Well its, i guess not the time to go out and get a beer" said Luther as he chuckled and turned to Jose. They both laughed it off as Luther told him that he worked with a group of friends on researching stuff for a university article that was headed by Professor Arthur Osborne, but they lost touch when he left the university and moved. He also told him that one person still works on this stuff and was very good at ancient folklore and dark magic and that he could get in touch with him.

As they shake hands as newly mutual friends, they both got up and exited the office bound on a mission to get answers from Luther's friend and expert in the field.

Tim Bennett looked nothing like a university professor of anthropology, with an appearance of a student instead and age to suit it. Jose was surprised when he met him.

He was really short and thin with ripped jeans and a skull and bones t-shirt marked voodoo crew; he wore a hat with it turned backwards and lots of bracelets of various varieties, some looking cultural while others seemed to be casual.

He greeted both of them and invited them into his home; they were lead to a room in the house that look like an office of ancient culture, or more so a museum of cultural antiquities with everything neatly in place. Jose looked around very impressed, as Bennett now seemed impressive with a touch of academic professionalism, he moved to his office chair and took a seat.

"So you are the guy researching the Tithonus machine" he said with a smile.

Jose replied with a sharp "yes" as he turned to look at Luther, Bennett got up from his chair and walked over to an armor where he opened a drawer and pulled out an old book.

He turned the pages as he walked back to his chair and sat down, looking up at both of them, he turned to Jose and said "You're in a lot of trouble here friend" as though

Jose didn't somehow know this but looked at him with a desperate look and asked "what can be done?"

Tony began to explain, "The machine is powered by a soul in exchange for a soul. Unfortunately, one of those souls will be replaced for the lucky one to take over the body of the replaced soul permanently.

The machine is based on the principle that an old dying person can exchange their soul with the body of a young healthy person by soul exchange. This takes time as the crystals that power the machine recharges slowly, after the death of the primary soul exchanger the secondary soul exchanger is prep for replacement by that I mean the person will undergo several life-changing events as their soul leaves their body and the new one enters.

After full recharge of the crystal the machine will begin the process of exchange but with certain distinguishing things, for example the person will over the period of time experience the torment of supernatural forces as the spirit is caught between conflicting worlds.

Towards the end, the soul giver will have their soul and present life ripped out of them".

As Bennett finished his explanations both Jose and Luther stared at him speechless with their eyes wide open. Then after a moment of silence Jose broke it asking "What am I to do now?" with a look of hopelessness in Jose's eyes.

Bennett said "Ok this is bad but my book doesn't say how its reversed especially if the person have already died, which from the look in your eyes they have, but my best guess would be to destroy the crystal in the machine to prevent full recharge and after the required period of time have passed the process will be permanently stopped".

"Simple as falling off a branch" he said with a smile.

"I have two days left Tim" Jose said "Well you need to get a move on then, find the machine, destroy the crystal before midnight on the last day and all is good" Bennett said while slamming the book shut.

Jose and Luther thanked him as they left his office and as they exited the front door, he said to them, that all things come from faith that shapes our belief, depends on how strong your faith stands it can be more powerful than any ghost story. They thanked him again as they left.

Luther gave Jose the reassurance that he was going to help him and that they will figure out a plan in the morning as they shake hands in agreement, it was late when they left Bennett, and they parted ways to head home for the night.

Jose came home with a heavy heart and lost the appetite to eat anything for dinner; he just made himself a cup of tea and drank it before he headed off to bed. He was in a deep sleep when all of a sudden he was awakened by a loud thump on his bedroom door, he could see from the outside light coming under the door crease that someone was standing outside the door.

He sat up in his bed with beads of perspiration on his face as he stared at the door, the figure stood motionlessly but then moved away.

The outside hall lights went out as Jose could hear footsteps walking coming up the corridor to the room. He saw the door knob turn but as a precaution he always closed his bedroom door, after several attempts to open the door a loud thump was heard. Jose asked who was out there but got no answer as the thumping got louder, suddenly the door flew open, and he was staring into the dark corridor.

He quickly jumped out of bed and reached picked up a cricket bat he always keeps next to his bed, arming himself with it, he slowly walked over to the open door, sticking his head out the door and looking into the dark passageway he could see nothing.

Not only did the darkness affect his vision but the dim light coming from the outside streetlights made moving shapes and shadows while at the same time provided low lighting.
Jose's breath a sign of relief as he saw nothing outside, he then lowered his cricket bat and turned around, standing in front of him as he turned was the grotesque crookedly bent figure of Doctor Don Lichtenstein with a horrifying smile on his face. He started moving crookedly and fast towards him, as Jose picked up his bat and swung a strong gust of breeze blew open all the bedroom windows knocking him off his feet and flinging his bat into the dark corridor.
He felt agonizing pain coming from his head after hitting it hard on the ground, then suddenly, he could feel something clutching his feet, as he raised up to see what had taken hold of him, he saw two crooked hands holding on to his feet, suddenly a strong pull of great force, and he was being dragged from the doorway and was being pulled under the bed.
He held on with all his strength to one of the bed foot, but the force was too strong pulling under the bed. All went dark and silent.

Day two

Jose woke up next morning on the floor, rubbing his eyes and head trying to remember what had happened but couldn't. The only memory that clouded his mind was that of a nightmare, one he quickly tries to forget while struggling to get up off the floor, he discovered excruciating pain in his joints accompanied by a back pain he hasn't gotten in years after a back injury working out at the gym.
Moving over to the kitchen, he discovered that the water had stopped when he turned the tap but as he stood looking into the sink tired and still shaken from the night before, the pipes suddenly started shaking violently. He moved back in shock, as he started at the shaking tap, just then blood came gushing out of the tap and filling up the sink.
Horrified at what he saw, he ran over to his night stand where his cell phone was and started dialing, he could see the name Luther on the screen.
Luther picked up the phone only to hear a panicking Jose at the end, he could barely understand what he was saying and could tell from Jose's voice he was really scared.
Luther told him to calm down and to meet him over at Bennett's, and they will try to figure out what's going on. As Jose hung up the phone he heard a voice coming from the kitchen, it sounded faint at first, but then a loud scream followed, this sent shivers down Jose's spine as he dropped the phone in shock. He stared at the open kitchen door now with pools of blood on the floor.
As he slowly moved towards the door, the glare of light coming through the kitchen window was in his eyes, but he could make out the figure of a man perched in a crooked fashion over the sink, the body was mangled and twisted, the face was white and pale, a sight that looked like death with blood running down his mouth.

"One more day now, just one more day" said the creepy figure with a crooked evil smile. Then suddenly it jumped off the sink and started crawling over towards Jose who while backing up quickly tripped over the carpet and fell on his back.

He rose up quickly after and could see the creepy figure now close to the door, he struggled to get up and just in time slammed the kitchen door shut. He could hear banging on the door, but it soon stopped. Jose got the bravery to walk back over to the kitchen door and slowly opened it. He looked inside the kitchen that was now very quiet and couldn't see the creepy figure anymore and the blood on the floor and sink was also gone.

Putting his hand over his face he began to cry, never in his life in all of his struggles had he ever gone through such an experience,

He didn't know if he was losing his mind or was he really battling a supernatural force out to get him.

Whatever it takes he realized that he needed to figure it out and get the situation under control, putting confidence in his mind and the same fighting spirit he always had in life and business, he slammed the kitchen door shut and headed off to the bedroom to get prepared.

Bennett was in a state of high euphoria when Jose and Luther walked in. "I'm glad you guys came back" he said while waving a piece of paper in the air. "From what you are telling me is a unique experience, spirits from all around is already sensing an opportunity for life again". Jose was more interested in a plan to destroy the crystal and stop all this from happening. Bennett back in his university days alongside his partner Arthur, were very good at breaking into the university archives to steal lab equipment for midnight oil work.

His plan to break into the Lichtenstein mansion followed a well-drawn out blueprint map of the mansion, where he got it from neither Jose nor Luther cared to ask but gave each other the look of amusement accompanied by a little chuckle.

He highlighted that breaking into this mansion was like breaking into the Royal Bank.

It was highly secured, from laser trip wire; to encrypted security code keypads attached to a large steal disguised trap door that keeps everyone from the machine, to highly train ex special force security guards and German shepherd guard dogs.

The mansion had more than ten security cameras, most hidden not to mention the many live in support staff. This Jose saw was not going to be a walk in the park but from the structure of the plan laid out, he felt relieved and very impressed by Bennett's breaking and enter skills.

Firstly, Jose would visit the mansion and claim that he needed to immediately speak to Ms. Lichtenstein about the insurance policy as a matter of urgency that can't wait another minute, this would take him in the hallways nowhere else, after Jose is in place, he would go around the front of the mansion and create a diversion, he highlighted how good his drunk man acting is and how it would distract the guards and dogs to the front gate at the west side of the fence security cameras will be focused on him as these are directional cameras controlled from their control room giving Luther the opportunity to jump the side fence and head to the pool house.

Once Luther got in the pool house, he handed him a piece of paper showing the electrical connection to the pool pump and with instructions how to hot wire the circuit to cause a well-timed fire.

Bennett gave a wicked grim as he said they are jerks anyway, so this isn't a bad thing. They all agreed and laughed; this cleared the tension Jose was feeling causing him to relax a bit.

After the fire starts, everyone would be distracted and will give him the opportunity to jump the west side fence, by that time he would have already slipped into a security guard suit and clip on a fake badge he printed out. After which he could enter as a staff and gain access to the control room and from there take over the security systems.

Bennett throws both hands behind his head with a big smile on his face and said "easy as falling off a branch", what would be now his winning catchphrase.

Luther said well the plan is set, while turning to Jose. Bennett said he would go over everything so by evening it should be perfect.

All the planning took a lot of time and by the end of agreeing on the plan it was already late afternoon. All parties were to meet up 7 pm when it was dark so that the night would give them the cover they needed.

The plan was set and everyone knew their roles, Jose thanked Bennett for all the help and putting his self at risk to help him, Bennett just nodded and said "Helping my fellow man is my greatest duty". Jose from that point had a lot of respect for him now that any time before, they left his house while he was about to start studying for his next great challenge, how to conquer his favorite video game.

As Jose drove up Luther's driveway a sudden sadness came over him, Luther picked it up and tried to reassure him by said "don't worry friend we are going to get through this, and you will be fine". Jose turned to him and said "I really hope so".

As Jose entered his house he could sense the cold feeling of death, windows were closed, yet he could feel cold breeze brushing his face, the dark hallways and dim light coming from the window gave him a feeling of dread.

As he stood motionless in the hallway, he started to think about how much he didn't do with his life and how much he wanted to do, he thought about all the times at the gym, he passed up an opportunity to find romance because he was always focused on work and the one true friend he had in college he never spoke to after they left. All the thoughts rushing through his mind felt like weights adding on his shoulder, so much that he sank to the floor with his back braced on the front door, his face in his hands; he started to cry once again.

Sometime must have passed as he fell asleep on the floor bracing the door, he was suddenly awoken by a strange eerie sound. He stared into the dark but couldn't see anything; he got up and switched on the lights in the hallway, when suddenly he saw something diving behind the sofa. He cautiously moved over to the sofa while picking up and arming himself with an umbrella that was left at the side of the door, with one sudden move, he swung the umbrella hitting the back of the sofa but saw nothing.

Furthermore, he smiled and breathed a sigh of relief; suddenly he heard footsteps running upstairs in his bedroom and the bedroom door slamming shut. Once again armed with his umbrella, he slowly walked up the dark stairway.

Clutching the door knob tightly and turning, he felt the feeling of fear; flinging open the door he could see with the mere light coming through the bedroom window from the streetlight, standing in the dark room at the foot of his bed, the figures of two small children a boy and a girl, their eyes were glowing white, their hands and feet looked skinny and feeble, but he couldn't see their face. Jose asked "What do you want?" Right after he asked he saw both children extended out their right feeble hands and pointed at him.

Dropping his umbrella on the floor, Jose ran down the stairs and straight to the front door, but the door just won't open.

The sound of children's laughter was heard from behind him as he slowly turned around to find both of the ghostly children standing behind him, the sight of them seen clearly in the living room light made him cry out in terror.

Their face was covered in blood and their eyes were gone, he could see blood running down their white night gowns that looked 17th century. Then one of them opened their mouth, he could see the black empty void that filled these nightmarish things but couldn't understand what they wanted from him or who these children were, if they had been some demon from hell sent to torment him or children who suffered a terrible faith very long ago.

He could hear a faint sound coming out of the open mouth of the boy and as he struggled to hear and understand the words, he could be sure it was saying "HELP US", just then the girl said "Do you see him, because he sees you". The lights in the hallway started to blink on and off as the children moved closer and closer towards him. He struggled to open the door, but then the lights went off, and the whole house was dark.

Day three

Jose was awoken by the sound of his phone ringing; he was lying in dirt and grass with his cloths wet and dirty. He was puzzled and confused as to where he was and how he got there.

Rubbing his eyes and looking around, he could see he was in some part of the countryside next to an old well.

He got up and looked around and saw an old house a few blocks up the trail.

His phone started to ring again, as he bent down to pick up his phone he could feel a lot of pain in his back again but one that knocked him off his feet.

Rolling around in pain on the ground he could feel trickles of blood coming down from his nose, right after which the pain went away.

Lying on the ground trying to come to grips with the nightmare he woke up to, the phone rang again, he picked up the phone and answered it, Luther in a worried tone was asking what happened, he came over to his house, and it was locked up tight and no one was home, he said he tried to call several times, but the phone kept ringing out.

Jose tried to explain to the best of his knowledge the stranger and unusual the whole situation appeared to both of them. He told him he didn't know where he was but was going to walk to an old house to see maybe if they have a car and can give him a lift back to town.

Getting up wasn't easy as it usually was because his body felt different, as though he was an old man. He managed to get to his feet and start walking towards the house. The cool breeze on the way to the house felt good on Jose's face as he lifted it up to the breeze, he forgot how nice and beautiful the countryside was as he spent most of his time in the city working.

At the door step, he tried to wipe away any blood from his nose and straighten up himself before he knocked. He could see on the mailbox as he looked around and waited for someone to answer the door the name Bells, and around the right side of the house what appeared to be an old abandoned barn that saw better days.

The house really was creepy but for Jose nothing is more creeper than what he went through for the past few days, and he really couldn't pick or choose as the next house was another couple blocks away, this one he said in his mind as he waited had to do. The door was answered by a pleasant middle age woman who asked how she could help him.
Jose struggled to talk but she interrupted by asking if he was in some sort of accident. He relied on "sort of yes, up the road", she said "oh my dear, I'm sorry to hear that, well come on in and sit down".
 As he entered he could see that the place was old fashion with a mid-60s design and furnishing, which he found very strange for people in this day and age, they even had an old floor model tube color television a classic antique.
As amused as he was, he was more eager to find out where he was and if he can get a ride back to town.
The woman returned and introduced herself as Betty Bell, after they got acquainted, he asked where he was and if she can help him get a ride back to the city. She told   him he was in Corn Grove, what use to be corn capital of the east until everything dried up and died. She informed him that she had already called Paul, he was the help hand on the property that was out fueling up at the gas station, he sometimes tends t o stay awhile to play chess with Curtis. Betty was very nice and polite, as she handed him a cool glass of homemade lemonade, she said that her husband was out, or he would have been glad to give him a lift. Jose thanked her as he handed back the   empty glass and told her what a lifesaver she was for even offering him the cold drink. Betty smiled as she turned to head to the kitchen something strange caught his attention. Trails of rice lined the doorways of the kitchen and even the main doorway. He wanted to ask but decided not to be rude.
An old ford truck pulled up in the driveway as he could hear the creak of the door opening and closing, Betty came out the kitchen and said "oh wonderful Paul is here". As Paul entered he looked at Jose and asked without a second's hesitation, who is he, what's he doing here? Betty tried to pull Paul in the corner of the room and whispered something to him; Jose could see Paul looking at him with a serious expression.

Paul came over to him and apologized by saying we don't really have visitors here, so please accept my apology". After Jose said "no harm done", he noticed Paul moving towards the keys he had dropped on the night stand.
"Well we better get a move on" said Paul. Jose without a second's hesitation got up and head to the door, as he tanked Betty and walked off, he overheard her telling Paul remember to stay in the city if it's late to travel back. Jose thought it was strange but maybe because night travel for poor old Paul wouldn't be a good idea.
Waving Betty goodbye, the truck pulled out the driveway and started up the road. The silence in the truck was broken when they drove past the old well; Jose decided to take the opportunity to strike up a conversation. "So what is up with the old well?" Jose asked with a smile on his face, he could see Paul wasn't friendly at all and the question only seemed to annoy him, especially with the response given. "That well is nobody's concern no more, nobody", after that, they both sat silently all the way to the city. He waved Paul goodbye as he drove off but got no response from him.
It was almost 7 when Jose met up with Luther and Bennett.
"Are we set?" asked Bennett in an anxious tone. "Yes" was the reply from Jose.

At the mansion the plan was informed, Jose approached the gate and was greeted by armed security guards, after stating his business one of them when back to the security hut and called and asked to speak to the butler, he turned and looked at Jose suspiciously before he hung up the phone. He waved to the other guard at the gate gesturing that it's ok for Jose to enter. Jose breathed a sigh of relief as the gates opened, and he was told to go up to the mansion.

As Jose stood in the hallway waiting, Bennett made his way to the front gate with a drunken man's stage performance. "Good evening my good man, is this the upper scale restaurant and bar?" At this time the security guards were out of the hut and at the gate, as Bennett raised his voice the dogs rushed the gate barking, he could notice the security cameras stopped rotating and focused on him, at this time Luther climbed the side fence and ran quickly to the pool house.

The guards had a hard time trying to get rid of Bennett as his drunken act was convinced he had the right address. Five minutes after the commotion, someone shouted FIRE! FIRE! At the pool house, seconds later a fire alarm went off. Right on time Bennett said in his mind with a wide smile on his face.

A large blaze of fire soured up at the side of the pool house, this confused the guards as they turned to see what was going on, Bennett noticed the security cameras turning towards the direction of the fire and the guards quickly entered the compound, as they pushed the button to close the gate and head off in the direction of the fire, Bennett quickly slipped through the gate and ducked by some nearby bushes next to the entrance, he quickly changed into a security guard uniform and clipped on a fake badge, after which he got up from the bushes and headed over to the security hut where he saw an electronic key card he quickly picked up and put into his pocket. Bennett walked up the entrance and signaled Jose, they both headed around the side of the mansion and opened the side door next to the pool house to let Luther in. "Easy and breeze, Bennett" said Luther. "Ok let's get to the machine" said Jose. "One more thing guys" said Bennett, "We need to disable the security system" he pulled out a schematic of the mansion; at this time Jose was thinking in his mind that Bennett was a pro at this. He told them he would signal them when he disables the system to come up to the room. He headed to a door on the second floor that knocked. Furthermore, he could hear a buzzed and the locks unlocking, a guard came out and asked "what is it?" He told him that the building was on fire and everyone is to meet at the assembly fire point as this was the orders given. The guard signaled another guard at the monitors and they both exited and locked the door.

As they walked down the stairs, Bennett ducked into a passage that lead down a corridor to another stairway and turned back, checking to see if the coast was clear, he headed back up the stairs and to the security room.

Using the key card he picked up from the security hut, he held it up to a black square space on the wall; a blue laser scanner scanned the card and unlocked the door. "COOL" said Bennett to himself impressed by the state of the art security system. Entering the room he could see dozens of monitors and switches.

Pulling out his schematic, he saw a bunch of codes he quickly entered on the computer, this disabled the system and shut off the security cameras. "SUCCESS" Bennett said to himself as he quickly exited the security room.

Luther and Jose saw the signal from Bennett to come; they then quickly headed off in the direction of Bennett. As they entered the doctors room, Jose felt a feeling of dread coming over him, his head started to swing around like a merry-go-round as he could see the room spinning, Luther asked if he was ok and Jose replied "I'm not sure" in a low tone. "Nuts it's starting" said Bennett, "we better get a move on". As they stood at the wall Bennett pulled out a small electronic gadget that looked like a smartphone but with a keyboard, he took out a screwdriver and removed the disguised light switch security panel on the wall, this was no ordinary security system as it had a number of complex connections. Bennett connected cable connectors from his device to some of them and entered a bunch of codes.

The wall of the great hidden room started pulling back, and opened. Jose was very relieved to see the room with the machine and soon after destroying the crystal he would have his life back again. Everything was going as plan but as they entered the room, they heard a voice that sent terror into their hearts.
"You are very cleaver I see, the others weren't" said the butler holding out a gun in his right hand. As they turned to face him, they could see a big smile on his face. "It's unfortunate that I'll have to kill the rest of you but as they say life goes on" the butler said coldly.

Bennett with his gadget in hand pressed a button that switched on the room lights, as the butler looked up with surprise, Luther made a plunge in his direction, knocking him to the floor, the gun fell to the floor and slid under the bed. Luther delivered a powerful blow to the butlers face knocking him out.

Suddenly they all heard a strange sound coming from the machine, it powered up, and the gears started spinning, they could see flashes of light coming from the chamber and the crystal stared to glow.

Bennett ran over to the machine and stared at it in amazement, "wow" he said as he stood looking at the machine. "Shut it down Bennett" shouted Jose. Bennett pulled out an explosive device that looked like a set of small battery pack and fitted it to the side of the machine where the crystal was using duct tape. Just then, the machine stopped and all was quiet. The machine was dark and silent with no movements from the gears, "What's going on Bennett?" asked Luther. "I'm not sure" just as Bennett answered an image appeared in the machine, it was an image of the doctor standing on both legs staring at them with an evil smile on his face. Then he slowly turned and stared at Bennett standing next to the machine. The doors of the machine suddenly opened and dozens of pale crooked hands came out from the door, grabbing Bennett and pulled him into the machine. "BENNETT" shouted both Luther and Jose. The doors were open and all they could see is darkness inside, suddenly, Bennett appeared, his hands first then his head and the half of his body, he clutched the doors of the machine as he was still being pulled by the ghostly hands, just then the doctor appeared again standing in the machine staring at Jose, Jose felt lighted headed after seeing him again and fell to the floor. Luther ran over to help Bennett. Clutching Bennett hands he shouted," Blow the machine Luther, Blow it!" The gears of the machine started back spinning again, beams of lights shone from it as the gears started to spin faster. "BLOW IT" shouted Bennett again, while still being pulled into the machine. Luther let go of Bennett's hands as he was pulled into the machine and disappeared into the bright blinding light. Luther pushed a small red bottom on the explosive device, he saw a flashing red light that indicated to him the explosive was ready but before he could made well his escape a loud explosion was heard pitching Luther away from the machine. Pieces of metal, glass and gears went flying through the air as smoke filled the room.

The machine and crystal was destroyed.

Luther could still hear a loud ringing in his ears as he struggled to get up off the floor, a sharp pain in his back caused him to stagger up while holding his back in agony. Looking around he could see rubble from the destroyed machine scattered all over the room. The big smile on Luther's soon turned into sadness for Bennett whose faith was sealed with the destroyed machine.
Looking around he saw Jose on the floor still passed out, he could hear the commotion from outside as the loud explosion attracted the security. Quickly heading over to Jose, he tried to revive him by shaking him several times. "Jose, Jose" said Luther frantically.
The first sign of life in Jose was his eyes opening slowly accompanied by the words "Luther". Laughter of joy came from Luther as he hugged him and said "it's good to have you back in the land of the living buddy". As Luther pulled Jose up off the floor and quickly headed to the locked bedroom door, he heard Jose saying from behind him "you got that right" in replied to his statement "we got to find a way out of here" said Luther.
Suddenly Luther heard two gun shots going off from behind him, BANG! BANG! Luther slowly turned around to see Jose holding the butlers gun in his hand pointed at him, as he looked down to his chest he could see blood soaking through his white t-shirt. "What the….." said Luther in a shaky voice as he fell to the floor. Staring up at the ceiling; he could see Jose standing over him with a smile on his face and the gun still clutched in his hand. "We destroyed it, we destroyed it" repeated Luther as he slowly closed his eyes and died.
As Jose looked around the room he could see the butler getting up off the floor rubbing his jaw. "Belgrade, call the police and report this intrusion" said Jose in a German accent. "Yes master" replied Belgrade speaking in German
"Oh and one more thing, do clean up my house as soon as the police is finish" said Jose in a German English accent.
"Yes master" replied Belgrade heading to the telephone to call the police.
Jose walked over to the bedroom mirror and stared deeply into it, while fixing his hair, he let out a chilling sinister laugh.

Part three

The Scary Joke

Everyone loves a good joke, just like the people in this story, who took a joke too far without knowing that some jokes can have far-reaching consequences. So laugh it up because this is a joke to die for.

"I told you guys I don't scare easily" said Pak "I had my fear gland removed from an early age" Pak said jokingly.

"Ok Pak but let me tell you, Alan is pretty good with scary jokes". Shola said.

"She's right Pak, last year he had me and the rest of the faculty scared senseless." said Chris.

"Well put it anyway you can only say scare jokes are outdated" said Pak.

"What's the plan for Saturday Pak?" asked Chris.

"Same old stay home and watch country westerns with a bowl of corn chips and cokes" answered Pak.

"Well I guess you sound like you can use some company this weekend then, huh?" asked Shola with a big smile.

"Don't mind, will just break out a bigger bowl of chips and more soda" replied Pak with a happy look.

"Great that's set then" said Chris "could use the out time".

"Hey speaking of the devil, here comes Allan now" said Shola.

"What's up gang?" said Alan.

"Your still with that Scooby-doo bid Alan?" asked Chris jokingly

"Well for your information Chris, it's a greeting now not a mystery, like your brain" replied Alan sarcastically.

"That wasn't cool Alan" said Shola with her eyes rolled up in disgust.

"Any way, what seems to have you all excited?" asked Alan.

"Well, were heading over to Pak's this weekend to chill" said Chris.

"Yea, want to come over? There's plenty of corn chips and cokes" said Pak.

"Sorry Pak but I got a date Saturday, with lovely Lola, and well just to mention you guys aren't lovely" replied Alan proudly

"Ok well you're lost" said Pak.

"I'll recover" said Alan boastfully with rolled up eyes.

Just then a student bumped into Allan accidentally, he was wearing a funny shirt marked my eyes are in the wrong place with a funny picture of a pair of crossed eyes. Allan annoyed by the accident shouted at the student and said "hey buddy your right; your eyes are in the wrong place, so watch where you're going". The student turned and gave Allan a cold creepy look, he then turned to Shola and smiled, ignoring Allan's comments, and he silently walked off without saying a word.

"Clown" said Allan angrily.

Shola was upset with Allan; she told him he really needed an attitude check, but Allan just brushed it off by childishly sticking out his tongue.

"Catch you guys later, I got work" said Alan as he walked off and headed to his car.

Saturday Night at Pak's

Three two liters of soda and three big bags of corn chips accompanied by a John Wayne, and they were all set.
A living room preparation was a tiresome task for Pak, who went all out to make sure that everything was set for the evening.

"Well I'm all set, time to call up the guys" said Pak.

Four hours later Chris and Shola arrived. To Pak's surprise, they both walked with a contribution to the evenings eatables.

Chris brought a jar of dip and Shola brought gram crackers that seems to go well with the type of dip Chris brought, not to mention the fact that corn chips will work together well with this new addition, Pak was most pleased.

"Great guys, you thought of everything" said Pak clasping his hands together.
"We just couldn't let you take the evening glory alone now" said Chris tapping him on the shoulder.
"How are acting classes Shola?" Pak asked with a smile.
"Hey turn that up!" Shola interrupted.

On the radio, the news report read a disturbing report that sent chills down Pak's spine. The reporter read, "Today the faceless killer struck again in the quiet community of Gem Haven, as two victims were found horribly mutilated in their homes, with the skin from their faces carved off. This is the second murder committed this month of this nature, as investigators name the unknown perpetrator "the faceless killer". Residence living in the Gem Haven community is asked by local authorities to lock up and stay indoors after dark, and to report any suspicious activity noticed in the area to the nearest police station". When the broadcast ended Pak reached over to his vintage classic style radio and turning it off.

"Terrifying" said Shola with a worried look on her face
"Yea, I'm kind of freaked out" said Chris.
"Well I mean this is Gem Haven, and to know that a killer could be right outside the door" said Chris.

Paks backed was turned to his friends while still clutching the knob of his radio, lost in a daze, hardly hearing what his friends were saying. It was evident Pak was disturbed by the report.

"Hey Pak, you ok?" Shola asked concerned.

Pak turned around with a smile on his face and said "sure let's get to the movie before it gets too late".
One hour and a half into the movie and Chris is already yawning.

"Man country westerns late at night is not my thing" said Chris as he motions to get up and Points to Pak's washroom, He moves sluggishly in the direction.
Shola shook her head in disappointment and said "You had to be the awkward one".
Chris just yawned and shrugged his shoulder while staggering off to the washroom.

"Hey Chris has been gone an awfully long time in the washroom" said Shola concerned.
"Knowing Chris, he either had too many dip or he just fell asleep on the seat" said Pak jokingly.
"Seriously, it's over thirty minutes, Pak" said Shola concerned.
"Ok ok, I'll go check on the big baby" said Pak laughing and shaking his head as he gets up from his easy chair.

As Pak walked through his living room hallway and slowly approached the stairway, Pak could see that the sitting room window was open; a gust of cold breeze hit his face as he remembered the radio broadcast. FLASHING BACK TO THE BROADCAST "keep all windows and doors locked up" the voice of reporter echoed in his mind.
Pak moved to the window and looked out, nothing but the darkness covering the bushes and lit streets from the street lights. As he closed the window, a reflection of a dark shadowy figure stood behind him, clear and visible from the window glass. Pak swung around briskly but saw nothing.
Pak smiled and said "I must be tripping"
All the way up the steps with confidence, Pak stormed over to the washroom with haste.
"Chris, I hope you remember to flush" he said laughingly.
Looking down on the ground, he saw seeping through from under the washroom door was a pool of red liquid that looked like blood.
"Hey Chris, you ok dude"? Pak asked nervously
No answer. Pak decided to turn the washroom door knob. It was open. Pak slowly entered and looked around. "Chris you in here?"
On the floor in a pool of blood lied Chris with a knife stuck in his neck, with his cold dead eyes staring up at him.
AAAAAAAAAAAAAHHHHHHHHHHHH Chris, Oh Chris said Pak as he fell to the floor.
His hands on his head as he struggled to get up and run down the stairs shouting "Shola, Shola the Faceless killer is here, we got to get out of here" Pak shouted panting for breath.
Looking around Pak could see that the living room was completely dark and the TV was off, Shola didn't answer. Pak started to get worried now.
"Shola, where are you"? Pak asked nervously.

Moving closer to the sofa, Pak's foot tripped over something very heavy and solid that caused him to fall to the floor. Lying in a pool of blood was Shola on the floor with her throat slit from ear to ear; the same dead eyes stared at him as the nightmare now sets in on Pak. Loud screams of horror came from Pak as he struggles to get up off the floor, he could feel his chest exploding from the inside. Looking into the sitting room he saw a tall dark figure, as it moved towards the hallway lights, the sight of a horribly disfigured face emerged.

Pak was up and running as fast as he could up the stairs and into his bedroom. Locking the door, He struggled to remove the blood soaked phone from his side pocket," OH MY…." said Pak in tears on the bedroom floor as he struggles to dial 911. There was too much blood on the phone as he tried to dial, Pak tries to wipe away the blood from the screen and dial again, just then……

The bedroom door flung open with a loud crash, the hinges and the knob went flying across the room as the Faceless killer stood in the door way with a large kitchen knife. Pak dropped the phone which then slid under the bed.
"Hello 911, how can we help you?" Pak could hear the operator on the phone which was now under the bed.

As the killer slowly moved towards Pak "PLEEEEESE d… d…do don't kill me" stuttered Pak with tears in his eyes "PLEEEEEESEEE" the tears streamed down Paks face endlessly. The killer now stood over Pak, with the knife raised in one hand, with one powerful blow, the killer plunges the sharp blade into Pak's face. AAAAAAAAAAAAAAAAHHHHHHHHH!

HAHAHAHAHAHAHAHAHAHAHAHAHA loud laughter was heard as the knife blade went into the handle. Fake knife, Pak staring at it confused.
More laughter continued as Alan pulls off the mask and revels himself to Pak.
"GOT YOU BIG TIME OLD MAN" said Alan continuing to laugh uncontrollably now.
"Alan", Pak said with a puzzled look. "Alan it it's you you" stuttered Pak in a trembling voice.
"Yea dude it's me along" said Alan still laughing.
"Hey guys, hey guys, come on up" said Alan like a side show announcer.

After this Chris and Shola came in with a smile. "We got you Pak" said Chris
They all started to laugh as Pak tries to settle his nerves and get up off the floor.
"You ok buddy"? Chris asked
"You should have seen his face man, priceless" said Alan jokingly.
"Ok enough guys" said Shola in a disgusted tone.
"Yea you got me good Alan" said Pak with a trembling voice.
"Great then, what to eat around here?" Alan asked looking around while heading towards the door.

Chris taped Pak on the shoulder and said "no hard feelings but you just got flushed, booya!"He said laughing with his two fingers pointing at Pak.

Pak laughed and said "yea you guys really got me good, I guess Shola's acting classes really showed up today".

After tapping Pak on the shoulder again, they exited the room.

Pak moved towards the mirror on his chest of draws and stared deeply into it. Still shaken, he could feel a sense of horror this time but not one out of fear, it was a strange and unusual feeling in the pit of his stomach, one that was taking over him from the inside out. Then suddenly his head started trembling violently like an earthquake, his eyes turned blood shot red as his lips quivered into an evil smile.

One hour later, Chris, Shola and Alan are outside on the patio, soaking up the scary prank they played on Pak.

"One for the records" said Alan.

"You're an idiot" said Shola angrily.

"What, we were all in on this" said Alan astonished.

"Yea and I feel like dirt, can't believe I let you talk me into this" said Shola.

"She's right Alan, he was really scared, and I mean Pak hasn't even come down from his room since. Bet he's probably upset" said Chris.

"Whaaaaat "Alan shouted.

"This mean he's angry, Alan" said Shola, "I think you should go and apologies to him"

"Yea, I agree" said Chris winking at Alan.

"Ok ok, if you guys insist" Alan said with rolled up eyes.

As Alan headed back into the house to find Pak an apology, he noticed an unfamiliar sight on the stair way, drops of blood leading all the way up the stairs.

"Oh great a double take now" said Alan jokingly.

"Come on this joke is getting stale, I'm sorry ok Pak" said Alan at the bottom of the stairs.

"Hey Pak, I said I'm sorry ok, come on down now" said Alan a little annoyed after he got no response.

After a waiting a while with no reply, Alan got a little worried.

"Hey Pak buddy, you up their?" Alan asked nervously as he slowly walked up the stairs.

The top floor was now dark as Alan walked to Pak's bedroom, he could see the door partly opened. As he pushed open the door, darkness filled the room with only the dull glimmer of light coming through the window now casting a reflection on the chest of draws mirror which now sets an eerie glow of dim light in the bedroom. Looking up he could see the bedroom light bulb was smashed. Alan saw Pak standing in front of the cracked mirror staring into it. He could also make out a knife in his hand with blood dripping down the blade and something on the floor that looked like pieces of flesh next to his feet.

"Paaak buddy, you ok?" Alan asked very nervously.

From the little light reflecting from the cracked mirror in the dark room, Alan gasped in horror as Pak turned to face him.

Pieces of flesh from Pak's face were cut off giving him a faceless appearance. Around the eyes and the nose were gone with the flesh around the mouth gone as well leaving a horrid mangled smile. Blood covered his face as parts of bone were now very visible. A HISSSSSSSSSS came from his teeth which no longer had lips. Alan who now stood frozen in shock and horror, As Pak slowly moved towards him.
 He muttered in a low trembling voice with tears in his eyes. "It was only a joke" "it was only a joke" he repeated.

Pak lunged forward, knife in hand.

AAAAAAAAAAAAAHHHHHHHHHHHHHHHHH!

Part four

The break down

Don't you just hate it breaking down in the middle of nowhere, without any cell phone reception and the nearest town or gas station is miles away, well I don't know about you but the woman in this story, is about to run her luck in an attempt to get out of a sticky situation all because of a break-down. So grab a spare tire and let's go for a ride into the unknown.

It's been three weeks since any sign of the seven missing loggers from Ben's logging camp. Anxious family members and the continuous pressure from the press only make matters worse for the new firm that has taken over the business interest, due to the mounting pressure production was halted.

"Idiot Tree huggers" said Mitch general manager and part owner of Ben's logging camp.

"I sure they had something to do with it" said Mitch.

"Are you sure about that Mitch? Tree huggers normally don't kidnap or kill anyone" said Collin Production Manager.

"Who said anything about them being dead? Replied Mitch

"Just speaking hypothetically Mitch" said Colin rolling up his eyes.

"Speaking of which, aren't they under close watch since the first three went missing last month", " it would be foolish to try something like this again" said Collin.

"Well it doesn't matter Collin, we are losing lots of money due to this hold up and we still have people to take care of, it's a shame we lost ten of our boys but we have to think about the company and those we have to account to" said Mitch.

"Your right Mitch" said Collin.

"With that in mind, I've taken the liberty to handle this situation out of the public domain" said Collin.

"How so?" said Mitch.

"I've hired Nina Watterson, private detective and expert in this field" said Collin.

"Really" Mitch replied surprised.

"Yes, she worked the Hamilton case two years back" answered Collin boastfully. "Ah the missing child case" said Mitch.

"Yep" replied Collin, "and she's perfect for this case", "all the outdoor experience and the discrete skills needed to wrap up this case quickly without too much attention" said Collin.

"Good work Collin" said Mitch with a pleased look on his face. "With this case wrapped up early, we should be back in production in no time" said Mitch.

"Got that right" Colin said with a big smile on his face.

Next morning, Nina arrived at 9 am on the dot.

"Early" said Colin to Nina with a surprised look.

"Like to be professional Mr. Colin" Nina said in a firm tone.

45

"Great then, I'm sure you got all you need from the file, anything else feel free to contact me directly"

"Got all I need thanks" said Nina as she got up and left Collins office.

"What a stocked up witch" Colin said to himself as he smiled and went back to what he was doing.

At 4am next day, Nina set off for her journey to the logging camp to start her investigation but on her way she decided to stop at a dinner and gas station to fill up for the long journey.

"You're not from around her are yah" said the waitress with a southern accent.

"As a matter and fact no I'm not" Nina said with a forced smile

"So what brings you to these part's missy?" asked the waitress, whose name was Pamela from her name tag. A common name for a waitress especially in these parts Nina thought with a slight chuckle.

"Look Pamela" Nina said while dragging her name. "I know your just trying to be friendly an all, but I'd rather just finish my coffee and sandwich ok"

"Oh sorry my dear, didn't mean anything by it" Pamela said looking embarrassed.

"Nah that's fine, and I'm heading up to Ben's Logging camp" Nina said while taking a sip of coffee."

"No offense again dear but why on earth would you want to go there" Pamela said looking at her concerned.

"Investigating the disappearances there" Nina said while biting into the sandwich.

"And they go be investigating yours too if you go" Pamela said while turning to go to the kitchen.

"Hey what you mean by that" asked Nina concerned.

Pamela turned around slowly and said "turn back and go home, you don't know these parts" Pamela said walking up to her slowly.

"This is forest country, no place for city people".

"Ok but all due respect, I'm a pro at this" said Nina confidently.

"Found the Hamilton kid a while back, rescued her from those deformed hillbilly family myself" she said proudly.

"Oh right the Galloway family; those cannibalistic devils got what was coming to them" Pamela said with a node.

"Yea they sure did" Nina said before drinking down the last of her coffee and eating the last remaining piece of sandwich. Getting up and heading for the door, she turned to thank Pamela and noticed a strange look of sadness on her face.

"You're such a nice gal, go home to your husband and kids" Pamela said with a sympathetic tone.

"Don't have either" replied Nina while walking through the door.

On the road, Nina kept thinking about the case and the first missing person's report. This was one about a father and son on a hunting trip in the Dune Lake Forest, eight months before the three loggers went missing. No traces after search was conducted and the words search called off kept floating around in her mind as she drove into night fall.

Nina's mind got more worried after a flashing light on her dashboard indicated her car was overheating.

"Piece of junk" she said angrily as the car slowly came to a stop with smoke emanating from under the hook. All her attempts to restart the car failed.

"Oh nuts, you got to be kidding me" she said with a sigh of frustration.

Reaching for her cellphone she discovered there was no signal. "Of course" she said while putting her phone into her bag. Looking out her car window she could see the darkness covering the forest with no streetlights along this stretch of road. The eerie sounds of the nights forest could also be heard, with some recognizable from nature films.

Nina was stuck at the middle of nowhere and in the dark of night. She noticed after sitting and waiting for several minutes that no other car had passed by and that ever since her break down the forest alive with all its nature sounds all of a sudden got very quiet, a dead silence, as though something even spooked the crickets in the grass. This made Nina push down the lock on all her doors and rolled up the windows.

"I'll just wait it out till morning, hopefully someone will pass, or I'll get a signal" she said to herself nervously.

Then all of a sudden she heard a loud thump from in front the car.

"What was that? She said to herself as she reached for the car headlight switch. No sooner had she flipped on the car headlight switch than a monstrous figure dashed from in front the car and disappeared into the nearby bushes. "What the…? Nina said jumped back in shock; she quickly picked up her handbag and pulled out her hand gun. Holding it up against her face, clutched firmly in both hands, she nervously peered out the driver side window now rolled up and then moved to the passenger side also rolled up, but saw nothing. Nina started to chuckle, "I think I'm losing my mind, this dark forest is getting to me" she said while putting down the hand gun to her side.

"All I need to do is keep my gun close and my car locked up, and I'll be just fine" she said to herself confidently. Switching off the car lights made her a bit nervous about her situation but decided she would keep a keen look out while saving her car battery. It was after midnight; Nina must have fallen asleep, only to be awakened by a strange sound from the outside of the car, it sounded like scratching. She sprang up gun drawn in hand. Looking around she could see nothing. Thinking to herself, it must

47

have been a bad dream, she lowered her gun chuckling as said "You need to get a grip of your self-girl"

Suddenly as she looked behind her, she could see headlights from an approaching car in the distance. "Yes finally" she said with a big smile "I'm rescued".

Cautiously opening her car door and exiting, she looked around but all she could see is the dark forest and the trees blowing in the wind, the cool breeze caused her to hug herself to get warmth. She went around the front of the car and tried to wave down the approaching car. A glimmer of hope came over her face as the car started to slow down.

A Ford F150 flew pass her but slowly came to a stop some distances away. Nina could see the driver looking out the driver side window and shouting "What's wrong lady?" Nina shouted back "My car broke down, and I need help".

The driver then stepped out and headed towards her. He introduced himself to Nina and offered to take a look at her car troubles.

"I should have a bottle of water in my truck and some spare oil, that should get you up and going" he said. "Oh, thank you, thank you very much, I thought I'd be stuck out here all night, good thing you came along" Nina said happily. The man nodded and smiled then said with a southern accent "much obliged Miss Nina" as he headed off to his truck.

Nina turned and went back to her car, when she heard a yell….AAAAAAAAHHHH! She quickly turned around in the direction of the truck. "HELLO" she said nervously. "HELLO, ARE YOU ALRIGHT?" she said with a trembling voice as no response came back to her. She could see the trucks front headlights on, the truck door was open but no sign of the driver.

Nina got very worried now as she reached in to her car to pull out her gun, she even took out her phone with intention to later try a catch a signal. As she approached the truck, she called out for the driver again, after receiving no response, she moved to the driver side door with the gun aimed. She could see blood on the car seats and drops leading around to the front of the truck and then into the bushes. There were even splatters of blood on the front lights. "What the………?" Nina said in shock.

Then suddenly she heard rustles coming from the bushes, as Nina continued to look, she barely made out a tall figure which stood up out of the bushes, a sound like a growling dog came from it as the eyes opened she could see two glowing dots. Nina let out a horrified scream while turning to run back to her car, almost at the door she tripped and fell once but got up back quickly to open the door and enter. Locking the door, Nina trembling in fear started to panic; she could feel tears come down her face as she tried to calm herself down. "What the Hell is that?"

Just then a loud crash was heard at the side of the car as it shook violently. Nina could see a dark figure at the passenger side door. Something was trying to get in; Nina started screaming, as she aimed her gun towards the door, BANG! The gun went off. The bullet shattered the passenger side window; just then, a loud cry was heard from the outside as the dark shadowy figure fell to the road.

Everything was now silent.

Nina still scared but convinced she had shot whatever it was dead; she then slowly moved to the broken passenger side window and stuck her head out cautiously.

To her horror, lying on the road in a pool of blood, shot dead was the driver of the truck. His stomach was torn open and his throat gashed. Nina started to scream as she looked at the dead body, as she looked up she could see a figure running towards her very fast. As she pulled back to the driver side of the car, the figure crashed into the car. This caused the cabin light to go out and the hinges from the passenger side door to give way and fall off.

Nina was staring into the darkness of the torn off passenger door, trembling in fear, she aimed her gun again towards the door, her hands trembling with fear; she could barely steady the gun.

Suddenly, CRASH! The driver side window was broken, and two long claws came through the window grabbing Nina. She started screaming as she struggled to free herself from the grip of the ghastly creature, in her attempts to free herself, her gun was flung out of her hand and through the passenger door.

Nina managed to drag herself across the passenger side door and slid her way out. Whatever it was that was trying to get her was now in the car and was trying to grab her leg. "Let gooooo" she shouted as she kicked at the claws. Falling flat on the road right next to the dead body of the truck driver, she managed to pull herself up and start running towards the truck.

She felt an excruciating pain in her right leg, this caused her to look down at the leg, she could see three bleeding claw wounds, that was very long and deep, trails of blood followed Nina all the way to the truck as she limped on one leg to move.

Inside the truck she looked all over for the keys but couldn't find it, "Noooo he must have taken it with him" the thought crossed her mind, could the keys be lying somewhere in the bushes or is it still on him. As she looks towards her car and the dead body lying at the side of it, she slowly realizes that she didn't have enough time to do searching when something is trying to kill her.

Just then, she heard rustling in the bush next to the truck, backing away slowly from the truck, suddenly a feeling of terror came over her as the sounds got closer and closer.

With one frantic rush, Nina turned and started to run away in hope to escape her stalker, she could hear charging footsteps behind her but didn't chance turning around, She just kept running.

Charging through the dark, cold and scary woods sent more fear in Nina's mind as she struggled to stay alive. She ran through some brambles which tore at her cloths and scraped her hands, feet and face, but she kept pressing on, until she tripped over a fallen down branch causing her to fall to the ground. With her back lying flat on the soft moist soil and her eyes staring up into the starry skies, Nina was in a lot of pain. CRACK! Went a branch some distances away, this caused Nina to get up quickly. Looking around the dark forest, she knows now that she's lost and with a monster chasing her, she doesn't know which direction to run. She heard rustling in the bushes at the back of her which caused her to panic and run in the opposite direction of the sound to get away.

Running for her life was no strange thing being a popular private detective, but this was one time she actually felt really scared, as thoughts about her life flashed before her, she quickly put them aside as she ran to stay alive. So far it seems like she may have given the creature the slips but just when she thought her worries was over, her feet slip off the edge of a steep slope causing her to tumble over and roll down the slope.

Falling to the bottom of the slope, her head hit a rock, Nina was groaning with pain as she held her head. She could feel fresh blood coming from a wound on her forehead.

Slowly getting up she could make out lights coming from a nearby cabin. A glimmer of hope rekindled in Nina as she started off running in the direction of the lights. She could now hear a rush of footsteps gaining on her as she now realized that the creature was still behind her and her only hope of survival was to make it to the cabin. Her athletic years in college paid off as she out ran the creature all the way to the cabin; she could hear the charging footsteps slowing down to a sudden stop. Reaching the cabin door brought ease to Nina as she banged on the door begging for someone to open the door.

Suddenly an elderly man holding a shot gun opened the door very annoyed. "What the hell is going on here"? He asked angrily. Nina didn't waste no time, she rushed through the door falling to the floor. "Lock the door, NOW!" she cried. The old man didn't argue, as he put his gun to his side and turned to close the door. "Now you want to tell me what the Hell you're doing on my property young lady?" he asked angrily now with his gun pointing at her.

Nina raised her hands in a waving gesture as she struggled to catch her breath. "I'm being chased by something out there, it already killed someone" she said trying to catch her breath again. The old man peering through the window but didn't see anything, he slowly turned to look at her.

"Look I can see you're lost and scared but nothing's going to hurt you now" he said with a puzzled look. He slowly went over the corner of the cabin and rested his gun down in the corner, after which he sat in an easy chair and turned to face Nina.

"I'd give you a lift in the morning, my boys took my truck, so I guess you can stay for the night" he said with a crooked smile. Nina thanked him as she struggled to get over what had happened to her.

The old man introduced himself as "Popper" and pointed to an old black and white picture in the living room which was his late wife. After Nina introduced herself, he got up and offered to show her to a room where she can refresh and rest.

He took her to a room on the top floor of the cabin and opened the door. He told her that she can stay there for the night and there's running water in the bathroom. Nina thanks again him for his kindness and hospitality, after which he said "no mention it" he then exited the bedroom.

Nina closed the door and went into the dark room. Reaching for the light switch, she switch on the lights, it was a small dusty room, with an old fashion style, even the bed and vanity was vintage, looked like something from the sixties. Thankful nevertheless, she headed to the vanity. Staring into the vanity mirror, she tried to wipe away drops of blood from her eyes and face.

Still in shock at what had happened to her and all she had just gone through, she still couldn't get out of her mind why anyone would be living alone out here, especially when people are turning up missing and there's a dangerous creature in the woods. Dismissing her unusual suspicions of Mr. Popper, she turned in the direction of the bathroom when her hand knocked over a box that was resting on the vanity.

Bending down to pick up the fallen box and scattered contents was very painful as Nina was very sore from her ordeal.

Picking up the contents, she could see it was jewelry and lots as well but one caught her eye.

As she raised it up to the light, she could make out the inscriptions on a gold chain, a pendant with the words "to my DAD Harry Rodgers, Happy Father's Day". Nina dropped the chain to the ground as she started thinking back at the first missing person's case in the area. The one about the father and son that went missing on a fishing trip, Harry and Paul Rodgers, terror once again came over Nina as she remembered the photo of Mr. Rodgers, he was wearing the chain the day he went missing along with his son, the big question now was, why Mr. Popper had the chain in his possession.

Nina cautiously opened the door and walked slowly down the stairs, she could see from the walls that there were no pictures of his sons he claimed to have taken his truck but as she thought it over, he didn't say it was his sons but his boys. Reaching into her pocket, Nina just remembered her cell phone, still no signal, she quickly put it back in her pocket and headed to the front door.

Just then, she heard a voice that cause her to froze in fear "Leaving so soon" Mr. Popper's voice was heard very loud from inside the living room. Nina jumped from shock while turning around very briskly. Standing now in the hallway, was Mr. Popper with his shot gun aimed, he had a devilish grin on his face as he moved slowly towards Nina with the gun aimed only to shove the gun barrel onto Nina's forehead. Nina closed her eyes in fear as she felt the steel barrel pressed against her head. "There, there now, I won't kill you" he said while lowering the gun. "You don't understand, but you will" he said with an evil smile on his face. He made a gesture to Nina to go over to the living room, after they entered, he ordered Nina to sit.

"What are you going to do to me?" Nina asked pitifully. Mr. Popper turned to face her, with his gun to his side, he replied "it's not me you got to worry about, it's them". "Did you know this was called the flour mill road before those idiot loggers took over these parts". At this time Mr. Popper was walking towards the window behind Nina and stared out into the darkness. Nina turned around to face him but as she listened attentively to him, she kept thinking of ways to get away or at least, a way to get the gun away from him.

"I used to be in charge of operations, born and raised in these parts". "Then one day, my family and I went out for a drive" he took out a picture of a little boy from his pocket and held it up in front of his face. "Must have been really late, didn't see a deer at the middle of the road, I tried everything to avoid hitting it. He lowered the picture and his head. "I just lost control" he turned to look at Nina; he had a sad look on his face. "Next thing I know we were…." He stopped talking and stared at the picture of his wife hanging over the lit fire place.

"I lost them that night, but faith would have it, I somehow survived, lost and wondering in the woods wounded and hurt, I was about to give up on life when they found me" he said and turned to her with a smile. "For some reason they didn't kill me, what happen next is what I would call faith". He walked over to the fire place and pulled out a key. "That night I lost my family but found a new one" he turned to face Nina holding up the key. At this time Nina saw a fountain pen lying on the table. She quickly picked it up as he turned away to look at the fire. She stood up with the pen hid behind her back. "I understand you had it hard, but this isn't the way, this isn't right".

He yelled at Nina "You don't understand anything, those darn loggers shouldn't have bothered them, they were just good hunting animals in the forest, and it's been years since….." he suddenly stopped but continued. "But now they got a taste, and they seem to love it very much". He turned to face Nina and said "I got to keep my children happy".

He started to walk slowly over to Nina with his gun clutched firmly in his hand.

Nina knows that trying to wrestle away the gun would not be wise but trying to escape and take her chances with whatever was out there was better than being shot. "This is the key to your freedom my dear, I'm sorry" he said as he held up the key again.

51

As Mr. Popper stood right in front of her, with the pen tightly gripped in her hand she made a lunge at him, jamming the pen right into his neck. Blood was gushing from the stab wound, as Mr. Popper let out a cry of pain; he dropped the gun and fell to the floor as he struggled to get the pen out his neck. Nina saw the opportunity to make a run for it, bending down to pick up the key to the door. She then ran to the door and unlocked it.

Now out the door, Nina was once again into the dark forest running for her life. "You can't get away" followed by loud laughter as Mr. Popper stood in the doorway. She ran as fast as she could in the pitched dark forest covered by big branches all around her. Nina could feel the burning pains from her wounds as her sweat fell on them.

Then all of a sudden, Nina felt the ground beneath her feet caving in as she fell through a large hole in the ground and landed on the floor of a cave. She may have passed out for some time, after she came too; she felt an excruciating pain in her leg. Struggling to find her phone she managed to shove in her pocket, switching on the flash on her phone, she examined her leg. She noticed a large bleeding gash with that indicated to her that it might be a broken bone, as she touched it she could feel bone sticking up. A cry of pain followed by gushing blood, Nina realized she was in a very sticky situation now.

Shining the light around the cave, she could see a large opening straight ahead. Still as she checked no signal, "of course" she said with a sigh of frustration.

Looking up she could see climbing out was very much now out of the question. Just then she heard a strange rustling sound coming from a dark corner of the cave followed by a few falling rocks.

Nina froze in fear as she held the phone up in front of her and slowly moved the light in the direction of the sound, as the light came closer to where the strange sound was heard she could make out a shadow cast on the cave walls. She could make out a crooked silhouette shape of a figure standing in the same spot. There was a look of fear in her eyes as she let out a soft cry as the light came an inch close to the motionless shadowy figure.

The light struck the face of the creature which let out a screeching nightmarish scream, the face of the creature looked like a mutated bat with large ears but with a human like body with hands and feet with claws for finger nails. It was hairy and very tall with a slender appearance and a crooked hump on its back due to its visible spinal cord. The teeth were razor sharp with foam coming from its mouth and the eyes were large and black.

The creature took off in her direction very briskly, Nina let out a horrific scream as the creature leaped high in the air and landed on top of her, she could feel the teeth of the creature biting into her back and the sharp claws sinking into her ribs, her cries of pain was muffled as her face was pressed into the ground. Nina struggled to get the creature off her and to find a weapon she could use to fight back.

Feeling a large rock next to her, she armed herself with it and turned to her side where the creature was biting, with one powerful blow, the creature was struck hard in the head. It let of a screeching sound of pain as it fell back.

Rock in both hands, Nina rolled over on top of the creature and gave it several blows to the head. She could see blood gushing out from the creatures head and hear the sound of breaking bone as the creature lay motionless on the ground.

Dropping the rock to the floor and picking up her phone now cracked and damaged but with the torch still working, Nina was on her feet running in the direction where she saw an opening. Dragging her broken leg was painful as she ran, especially when her foot hit against rocks on the ground, she would let out a cry of pain. Suddenly she could feel herself falling to the ground as her phone flew through the air and landed some distances from her.

She had tripped over a dead body, she came to realize was the truck driver who tried to help her on the road, she quickly muffled her screams of terror. Looking around she could see from very dim light coming in the cave, she was in some sort of feeding ground. Dead and decaying bodies lied all around her; some were skeletal remains while others were partially eaten. The stench filled the air as Nina held her hand over her nose.

Looking in the direction where her phone fell, she could see the light was still on but then out from the corner of the wall in the cave a creature came out and was standing over the phone light, seconds later more came, she could make out four. The light seemed to be irritating the creatures as they screeched and screamed at each other, then one of the creatures hammered its fist into the phone with one powerful blow, smashing the phone completely and knocking out the light.

Nina laid motionless as she watched the creatures in the dim light returning to where they came from, she then noticed more creatures lying around as they went back to join them. In a quiet and peaceful fashion, huddled together in a sleeping position the creatures when back to sleep.

She noticed looking around the cave that there over twenty of them, families of these creatures and babies huddled together asleep.

Just then she saw where the light was coming from in the cave, it was an opening in the cave that appeared to lead out the cave. She crawled slowly as not to draw attention to the sleeping creatures she was surrounded by in what was there feeding grounds and living quarters. As she entered the opening she could see wrecked cars, trucks and bikes from various eras, some even going back to the early 1900s. It slowly dawned on her that these creatures were hunting people for many years with the aid of people like Mr. Popper they went undetected and discovered all this time because moving these vehicles weren't the work of these creatures. She could also make out a jeep with the words green tree. This was the truck the environmentalist drove when they went missing. Another truck with the words Ben's Logging was also there and even a sheriff's car. Just beyond the wrecked vehicles a small crawl space leading up an out the cave.

Nina lowered her head with relief as she continued to move slowly and silently towards the crawl space. Being cautious not to draw attention or wake the sleeping creatures.

Suddenly a car alarm when off when she jammed the door passing it. All the creatures jumped up with a loud angry growl and looked in the direction of the alarm.

Nina spared not a single second, she was up on her feet in a hurry to get to the crawl space, dragging her broken leg, she quickly scrambled and clawed at the dirt in the crawl space to make her way up, hearing the creatures now in the car lot, she continued with heist until at last she was out.

It was daylight now; she could see the morning sun coming through the trees and felt the heat on her face. Nina took off in any direction with heist, dragging her broken leg.

She was now in a frantic and confused race to get away, running and screaming for help. Suddenly she saw the road through some trees up ahead and started off in the

53

direction. At last, she was out of the forest and on the main road. As far as she could see, she was not pursued by any of the creatures.

Nina battered, bruised, broken and bashed stood on the road looking around crying out for someone to help her. Tears fell from her face mixed with blood as the confused, scared and exhausted Nina cried uncontrollably.

SUDDENLY..............HOOOOONK! A loud truck horn was heard from behind her as she turned around, SLAM! The truck struck her, tossing her up into the air, her body hitting the side of the truck before falling dead on the road.

The mangled blood soaked body of Nina lay on the road as the truck driver stopped the truck and came out to see what had happened.

Written at the side of the truck was the company name 'Ben's Logging's.

Part five

The 911 call

In the event of an emergency, 911 is the best and most frequently called number in a crisis, but the caller in this story will need much more than 911 to save them as the first responders are now about to be plunged into a nightmare of their own.

"Hello, hello ....pleeeese hello" said Mary Walters, devoted housewife and mother.
"911emergency, how I can help you madam?" asked the operator.
"There's someone into our house" said Mary in a trembling voice.
"OK, madam, are you alone?" asked the operator.
"NOOOO" said Mary with soft crying.
"My children is in their room and my husband when outside to see what's wrong", "I heard him crying out in pain then falling to the ground" said Mary crying louder now.
"Ok madam, stay calm and don't go outside, keep your door locked, and we will send someone over right away". The operator said.
"IT'S **trying to get in**" Mary said silently with soft crying.
"IT'S **trying to get in**" she screamed so loudly the operator was forced to pull off her headset.
"Hello, madam, Hello madam, are you there?" asked the operator.
The phone line went dead.

Fifteen minutes later, a police squad car pulled up in front the house with two uniformed police officers exiting the car.

Officer Crag Monty and his partner officer Lisa Bell approached the door with caution, looking around for anything suspicious.

"Hello, this is the police" said Crag several times knocking at the door.
"No response" said Lisa.
"Go around the back and check it out" ordered Crag.
"The door seemed to be locked from the inside" said Crag to Lisa as she left to go around the back. A few seconds later.......
A loud crashing sound was heard from the upper flat.
"Alright" said Crag, kicking down the front door and entering the hallway.
Seconds later, Lisa also kicked down the back door and entered.
"What's going on here"? Lisa asked. "These doors were all locked". "I thought they said this was a break in" Lisa said looking around puzzled.
"I don't know, but let's split up and search the house" replied crag.
Lisa looking around the living room and study, found the first shocking sight of Mr. Walters lying on the floor in a pool of blood; a quick check revealed that he was dead.
Crags cautiously moved up the top floor, while walking up, he found on the floor a strange white power scattered all over stairway, as he cautiously approached the doorway of the children's room, the shock and horror caused Crag to gasp.

"Hey Berta, checking up on the Walters case" said Crag.

"Sure Crag, I'll buzz you in" said Berta with a smile while moving to the evidence room door lock switch.

"Stuff is in two boxes on W 203" said Berta now moving back to her desk slowly. Berta was fifty-five and still waiting for retirement but seem pretty comfortable just sitting and waiting it out in the evidence room for now.

"Thanks Berta" said Crag walking into the evidence room.

Rows of shelves stood before him as he searched for the W section, under dim light in the room, his eyes slowly adjusted as he moved through the rows. Finally, he came up to the section and saw the boxes.

Looking through the boxes, Crag picked up a blood stained diamond ring belonging to Ms. Walters and gold Rolex belonging to Mr. Walters, he came to the conclusion that they were definitely not financially struggling, especially after looking at the life insurance policy Mr. Walters took out three months before his demise.

All the documents were well filed together and placed in order. They were organized in sections for easy finding. This indicated to Crag that the Walters were very neat and organized people.

"Never know this sort of money existed" said Crag jokingly to himself as he looked at the amount on the policy.

The white powder caught his eyes, picking up a tiny sample on his figure, he looked around nervously to see if anyone was looking, the coast was clear as he put the tip of his finger with the white substance into his mouth and tasted.

"MILK POWDER" said Crag to himself surprised.

"So it's not drugs" he said to himself.

In the collection bag there was something else, it had a yellowish appearance. Crag took a sample of it and placed it into a sample collection bag he was carrying with him, he then placed it into his pocket.

At the evidence room door he said goodbye to Berta who responded with the same pleasant smile as he left.

At the crime labs, he took the yellowish sample to the most trusted person he knows there, an old friend he once was best friends with and very best friends, actually.

"One whole year and here you are asking me for something" said Keisha crime science technician.

"Keisha, I really need your help on this please" said Crag in desperate tone.

"At least a phone call to see how I was doing or a simple hi every now and again" said Keisha upset while closing a lab report folder.

"I know it's over, but we used to be good friends you know" she said as she walked up to Crag and took the sample. She stared in to his eyes with a sad look.

"We still are Keisha, I trust you most in this world" said Crag in a gentle tone, he smiled as he stared deeply into her eyes.

They stared into each other's eyes for a while in an awkward silence.

"Right, what we got here" Keisha said while moving away with the sample.

"Don't know? I need you analyze it for me".

"You got it friend" she said with a smile "say after this you owe me dinner" she said biting her lips as she glanced at Crag and moving away to the bio room.

"You got it friend" Crag said with a smile as he turned and headed out the door.

Next day, Crag asked Lisa to collect the 911 call record made by Ms. Walters the night of the murders as well as to run a check on Mr. Walters background. Crag moved away from Lisa before she could ask anything but told her he was going to interview the Walters neighbors.

The interview with the Walters neighbors didn't prove much help at all, except one, an old lady who lived at the back of the Walters.

She told crag that the Walters were quiet people but Mr. Walters started acting strange ever since he came back from visiting a South American country in the Caribbean. She said "sometimes late at night he would be in his basement, she could hear digging and things knocking down", it used to wake her out her sleep, so out of curiosity she decided to one night investigate what was going on. Looking out her window she saw the basement light on and what appeared to be one of the Walters children with him. Very strange she thought, but they were always nice to her, so she never minded them or complained.

"Children", Crag said as he thought about the one lone survivor, the Walters youngest child. Crag never got his name, but it was something that was now on his list of things to check into next.

At the Caroline's home for children, Crag spoke to the nurse taking care of little Peter the Walters youngest child and only survivor.

"All he told us was his name and what he wanted to eat, nothing else" said the nurse.

"Did you try any form psychological approach" asked Crag

"Yes we did, Dr. Kenton spends a lot of time with him alone but got nowhere" replied the nurse.

Crag wanted to ask to see him but reconsidered after remembering the child's state the night he found him.

Hiding and scared for his life after seeing his family brutally murdered, he thought it might be pushing it, plus he thought it was dark, and he was hiding under the bed, so he still might not provide much help anyway. The look the nurse was giving him made him feel uneasy, it was one that indicated to him that he has worn out his welcome, after all the child did went through the worst. The one thing that ran through his mind though is why no member of the Waters family came to claim him after they were told about the murders and the one surviving child, it seems unusual no family haven't stepped up to take care of the child.

As these thoughts raced through Crags mind he moved slowly to the door to exit.

"Oh one more thing nurse, what did he ask to eat?" Crag said while turning away from the door with a silly smile, thinking it was a silly question to ask but decided it won't harm asking.

"Milk and Bananas, very weird, but that's all he'll eat" she said as she shrugged her shoulders and walked away.

Crag found this indeed odd but brushed it aside and exited the home. While heading to the squad car he glanced up at a window on the top floor of the home to see little Peter looking at him from the curtains. Crag smile and waved at him but he stood looking at him with a cold and serious look on his face. After the cold response from Peter, Crag entered his car and drove off heading back to the station to check up on Lisa's progress.

Back at the station, Lisa sat at her desk and paid less attention to Crag when he walked in, he walked up to her briskly.

"Hey got anything" he asked anxiously.

"GOOD DAY! to you too and yes" she said in a sarcastic tone as she handed him a brown envelope containing the 911 tapes. Crag collected it with a look of embarrassment.

"Also info on Mr. Walters is in there" Lisa got up from her desk and walked away from Crag, he could see from the look on her face that she was upset. "Thanks" Crag said as Lisa headed down the stair way.

Going over the 911 tapes of the call Ms. Walters made no much sense except of one thing.

"IT'S TRYING TO GET IN" Mary said before the line went dead. "What does that mean?" Crag said to himself. The mystery got even deeper.

Looking at Mr. Walters's lifestyle, Crag saw an average Real estate agent, earning an average income and a few extra on commissions but noting to afford an extravagant lifestyle, the Walters had a multi-million dollar life insurance policy and lived above average.

There was something interesting though, the trip to South America paid for not by the company but by one of Mr. Walters clients.

An Arthur Osborne, it seems Mr. Walters sold him a house a few months ago, single associate's professor moving from the city looking for a fresh start and got a perfect deal on the house and as part of his commission; Arthur tossed in a reward trip. Nice guy Crag thought.

A check with the airport baggage records would reveal that Mr. Walters's baggage was slightly heavier than his departure. "He came back with something" Crag said to himself in a surprised.

"Wonder what he brought back?" Crag said curiously to himself.

Checking with baggage security and customs office, Crag discovered that Mr. Walters brought back an old Scottish Ale bottle that was traded by the Dutch during the 14th hundreds, a rare antique type made out of ceramics, certainly attracting a fine price, but nothing valued over five thousand US dollars.

The bottle bared an inscription of some sort claimed the customs officer, a capital B was visible but the rest he couldn't make out due to the age of the bottle.

Crag asked the customs officer if he brought some pictures of those types of bottles, if he could identify it, in his mind the bottle may later on come in handy as evidence. The customs officer agreed that he could and with this Crag took out his phone and researched old antique Dutch bottles. "It's that one, I'm sure of it" said the customs officer pointing to a picture of an old antique bottle with the inscriptions written in Nigerian.

Crag thanked the customs officer and headed off to the University of Anthropology and Cultural History to have a better analysis of the bottle.

At the university he was greeted by a middle-aged woman of Native decent with a Caribbean accent. "Heard you had a questions about Dutch bottles found in the Caribbean" extending her hand out to shake Crags.

She introduced herself as Ms. Louise Fox professor and head of the Department of Cultural Anthropology.

"Yes that's right Ms. Fox" Crag replied while shaking her hand.

"I would have put you on to our Associates professor Arthur Osborne, another expert in the field, but he's no longer with us" Fox said with a pleasant smile on her face.

Crag remembered him as the one who paid for the trip Mr. Walters took to the Caribbean.

Entering Ms. Fox office, he could see many varieties of cultural artifacts, with similar looking Dutch bottles and Paintings of the Caribbean country sides. They were rather beautiful Crag thought, looking at the artwork and how well painted they were.

"Arthur was a bit eccentric but very good in the field" said Ms. Fox as she gestured to Crag to take a seat.

He then took out the photo of the Dutch bottle the customs officer identified and handed it to her, he apologized for the poor quality of photo as it was an internet print out and not a photo of the original artifact in question.

After examining the photo Crag showed her, Ms. Fox became deeply troubled and uneasy.

She told Crag that these types of bottles were bought by the Dutch from the Scottish to trap and keep very power spirits, they were mainly traded in a country called British Guyana in South America and was used because of its unique ability to preserve and keeps things, it keep water cool because of its porous clay nature and of course to be the perfect vessel to contain a spirit.

She continued speaking while searching through an old book she took from a shelf. This particular bottle holds a very powerful Demon called the Bacoo initially of Nigerian origin but was adapted into Guyanese folklore as a creature with the appearance of a little child, mainly of African descent but was known to change its appearance to other races; it can speak other languages and live mainly on a Milk and Banana diet. It can also bring fortune to those who find and release one from its vessel, sort of Genie some may call it, but its anger is ferocious especially if it doesn't get what it wants. The creature must be feed at a certain time and its preferred diet, once done, the owner would be rewarded with wealth and even wish granting, the creature is said to be very intelligent and very ancient and can be very devious especially if it's angry or doesn't get what it wants.

Folklore has told tales of entire families being killed in the Barcoo's rage and even villages held hostage until the creature is satisfied.

Crags face turned pale with fear at what he was hearing, he was in complete disbelief.

"It can't be, it just can't" Crag said while shaking his head.

"If you ever encounter a Bacoo and it's lose from its vessel, you must trap it back into its bottle or the spirit will be allowed to walk free" said Fox with a concerned look.

"What happens if it's allowed to walk free?" asked Crag with a worried expression.

"It's a deceiver of men and can seek other families, only to repeat the same process over and over again" said Fox as she's slamming her book down with force on her desk, this surprised Crag causing him to jump from his seat.

After the conversation, Crag got up from the chair speechless, it took a while before he could say thank you while heading for the door.

"One more thing, the bottle is its only home, saying the words Bacoo return home with the bottle in front of it will cause it to return, after this the bottle must be corked and buried". Fox said. Crag thanked her again and left.

With a worried expression on his face, he sat at his desk at the station going over all he just heard, Lisa walked up and stood in front of his desk. Lost in thought, he didn't notice her standing in front of him. "The chemical analysis report you requested is back from the lab" she said holding out the yellow folder.
"You were out when it came in" she said dropping the folder on his desk.
"Thanks Lisa, I guess I owe her that dinner now" Crag said with a simile relieving the tension on his face.
"Want to tell me what's going on?" Lisa said with a puzzled look on her face.
"I don't fully know yet Lisa, but I'm about to find out soon" he said as he picked up the folder and opened it, an envelope with the lab report was inside.
"OK but be careful, you don't know what you're getting into, and you're going into it" Lisa said concerned.
"Thanks Lisa I will" he replied with a pleasant smile.
As Lisa walked away, Crag opened the envelope and read the report.

BANANA!

Crag shouted this out so loud that the whole top floor of the station looked around surprised, Crag sprang from his chair and started to ran down the stairs rushing pass Lisa, who asked if he was alright, he gave no response as he raced to the door and exited the station.

At the Walters residence the crime scene do not cross tape was still around the house and on the door.

Crag called the children's home to check on Peter, after hearing that he was asleep since it was seven in the evening by the time Crag got there, he proceeded to remove the tape from the door and enter the house.

Walking through the living room he noticed something they all missed.
"No pictures of Peter are on the walls" Crag said shining his flashlight on the walls.
No wonder no one came for him Crag thought.
His thoughts ran back to the interview with the neighbor about the late night basement digging. That's where he was going to start looking.
In the dark basement the only visible light was seen coming through the small window in the corner next to the washing machine. A cold breeze was felt surrounding Crag, one that made him shiver. Looking around the dark room with his flashlight brought back memories of the Walters last night alive and what the Bacoo did to them in rage of having his milk spilled and not being prepared on time. The price for a fortune was just too great he thought to himself.

A fresh patch of dirt on the floor attracted Crags attention. "This is where he was digging" Crag said to himself.

Heading over to have a better look, he could clearly see floor boards removed. Looking around, he saw a shovel at the corner of the room.

Grabbing it, Crag began digging with much curiosity. The flashlight securely rested on the dryer, now shinning directly at the hole Crag just dug.

Looking down at the large Dutch bottle with the words Abiku confirmed Crags worst fears, especially when he picked it up and looked at it closely.

"The cork came off" he said holding the bottle up to the light. "I got to find the cork" he said in a frantic search around the room.

Suddenly the door to the basement slammed shut.

Crag jumped in shock and looked around to see a dark shadowy figure standing at the door looking at him. In the dark he could only make out the shape and height but nothing else.

"PETER" Crag said softly in a trembling voice.

The dark shadowy figure started talking down the steps slowly and towards Crag. A soft growling was heard coming from the creature as it approached.

Crag desperately tried to find a way out of the basement as he looked around, but the only window was by the washing machines now behind the creature.

"My gun" Crag said loudly now discovering that in his mad rush to exit the station, he forgot his fire arm in the drawer of his desk. His last attempt he thought "I'll try trapping the spirit in the bottle and use something to cork it". Crag held out the bottle in front of the creature, and before he could say anything, the creature let out a loud scream, one Crag never heard before. It was so loud that Crag tried to cover his ears.

As Crag was slowly backing away with his hands covering his ears, he tripped over the shovel left on the ground falling backwards; the bottle flung from his hand and was tossed into the air, it then fell to the floor with a loud crash. Crag was now cornered with no way out.

As he got up from the ground and looked at the broken bottle. Hopelessness started stepping in now as he turned to face the creature, he could see it coming towards him slowly, the face partly visible now, he could see the unnatural look of something not human but a monster with the appearance of a child. He turned his back to the creature as it approached and faced the bare basement walls.

Crag closed his eyes, as he could feel the cold breath of the creature on the back of his neck. He felt it getting colder and colder as creature came closer and closer.

"I Know what you are" Crag said in a trembling voice with his eyes closed as the creature stood directly behind him. "I know what you are" repeated Crag.

The flashlight when out and all was dark.......

Part six

Psycho at large

The thought that a serial killer is on the loose in your hometown would make anyone scared but what about having that serial killer living right next to you. Well, that's the bases of this story, so be good and kind to your neighbors and don't forget to lend a helping hand.....literally.

It was Saturday morning and all was quiet in Hope town as usual, a peaceful small town with a population of 1862 people, not much ever goes on here and everyone is friendly and helpful. So was the norm with small towns where everyone knows each other and neighbors are actually nice. All that changed the day he came to Hope town. Oh, by the way, my name is Trevor Seamore, Hope town's handyman, part-time fix it, General store clerk and all over slave. Don't get me wrong though, I like it no other way, peaceful, quiet and serene but most of all normal.

I was awakened earlier than usual to the sound of a moving truck at 4 am, which was unusual for someone to be moving here at that time in the morning, anyway I got up curiously and when to the window to see what was going on. From the window with the blind pulled slightly, I could see from the well-lit street bright from the streetlight that illuminated it, that the vacant house across the street was getting a new occupant. I didn't even notice the for sale sign outside the property was gone.
A tall figure of a man in his mid-30s stood at the back of the truck unpacking his stuff, the driver asked on several occasions if he needed help but every time he would wave reluctantly at the driver and I noticed from where I was spying, rolled up his eyes in frustration, the last time with a forced smile and a sharp response "NO....THANKS". Pulling back behind the truck, he continued to unpack and set everything on the walkway to the house.
After everything was unloaded, he slowly crept up next to the shocked and surprised driver who didn't even noticed he was standing next to him. "Thanks" he said handing some money to the driver and slowly walking away.
The driver shrugged his shoulder and drove off. Standing facing the load of work in front of him, the stranger gave me the creeps, to be honest, I never saw a man that weird. While I was looking on, the stranger slowly turned and looked at my window where I was standing. Fighting to duck in the corner and pull back the blind, the thought hit me, that this guy is very unusual.

It was 6 in the morning and everything was bustling in the town. Getting around to making breakfast and preparing for work was my norm but today looking through the window to see what's going on next door was my first plan for the morning. To my shock and surprise, the sidewalk to the house was cleared and all the stuff moved in overnight. It must have taken a lot of work moving all that stuff, especially the large trunks. Man this guy was weird and quick, I thought to myself. Nevertheless it was work time, so I got to preparing and left home on time.

It was work as usual at Matt's Hardware and General Store, we got everything you need was his motto. Good old Uncle Matt, a fifty-year running family business and one that the town appreciates especially when its credit time.

This sort of consistency is what made him famous, back in the days, he used to be called the man of the hour, he always had what you needed and when you required it and at a reasonable price too.

Remembering the old times bring me back to Sunday school, especially the Sunday school teacher Mary Sketchand, beauty and graceful were her normality's as well as being direct, especially with me and my futile attempt to win her affection. She had other plans I guess, heard she got married to a rich city guy name Walters, Some real state business he owned or something. I hope she's living well and happy nevertheless.

Everybody that came in was all talks about the new guy in town, especially the women. Sounded like the frantic excitement over the mystery of the new man and the fact I did notice he wasn't bad looking either, not that I was paying attention.

Ooook, I even hear one say "if he's single there ready to mingle". My rolled up eyes expression caught the attention of one of them as she quickly changed the topic and asked about the sale on our packaged dairy products. A good one too, buy the package and get two free tins of canned milk, so you could get your eggs or cheese with milk at one wholesome price. Good job Hope town dairy farm I thought, they really pulled that one out of the bag and got a great response to this promotion too. Grabbing her change with a rude look on her face, she stormed out the store. At least she had manners to say have a good day.

Uncle Matt was in the store packing up a shelf when he called me over. Something he rarely did since he's very particular about his shelves, he likes everything to be specific in the chronological packing order, and after all he's been doing it for many years he always reminded me.

"Heard you got a new neighbor" said Matt.

The question annoyed me but yeaaaaa. It was like Jesus came to town or something. It's not often we get people moving here, so I can see why everyone is so curious about the new guy. My short response told Uncle Matt it was time to move on to brighter things.

"Anyway, I got a delivery to make to Ms. Alder" said Matt.

One of those packaged dairy products of course. Uncle Matt pointed over to the corner where they were packed. Ms. Alder, young, beautiful, pleasant and most of all single, I've been trying my luck for a year now, and I actually think I was getting somewhere. Only last week when I when over to fix her porch light, she told me she likes having me around, and I did notice a lot of orders placed for deliveries lately, noting that I would bring them by.

I anxiously picked up a package from the corner and headed on over to her place. Over at Alders place, I got a warm greeting, one that was accompanied by I'm glad to see you.

My excitement meter when up to high when she invited me in and asked if I'd like a cup of coffee? I said yes without a second's hesitation and entered her living room.

A neat and organized living room said a lot about Stephanie Alder, a single, hardworking woman who found the time to do housekeeping and look as good as she did. I knew I was right to admire her.

She brought a mug of coffee, a cute crafted one I may add then she invited me to sit in a recliner chair that faced the television. All smiles about the progress rapidly went away when she asked about my new neighbor, she heard everybody talking about. She was asking a lot of questions, if he's single, if he works around the town and if I spoke to him as yet. She highlighted as the towns man, I always had a keen ear about what goes on.

Fighting the sadness, I pulled up a smile, boy did that hurt, anyway i said "to be honest Ms. Alder I really don't know much about him" I emphasized the Ms. Alder part since it seems that's all I guess she could ever be to me.

"Oh, well ok, if you hear anything, just let me know" she said, as she quickly turned away her face from me. "I don't get out much you see" she said looking down to the floor in silence.

It was a clear indication for me to thank her for the coffee and leave, which I did after the three minutes of awkward silence.

The way back seem like a long one, my mind racing over my lost battle to win Stephanie and the fact that this new and unusual fellow seems to be getting high attention buzz. Not that I was jealous or anything..........well just a tiny bit ok!

Anyway back at the store it was work as usual. As soon as I got in, Uncle Matt took off leaving me with a line of customers at the counter. Errands he said he had to run, plus a request from the barber shop owner who was the town's only barber, to come over and help install new barber chairs. Hate doing that, honestly. I remember when he got the old ones, screwing down those chairs took me a lot of time.

Dealing with customers didn't seem like usual today for me, going over my corrupted thoughts about the events that took place earlier. One customer made it worst, she said "hey daydreamer, stop dreaming and start doing". It had so much meaning when I started to process it, and boy did her words stung me hard but for right now she just wanted her dairy product package, and I was really anxious to give it to her.

The sooner she got what she wanted the sooner she could leave. She gave me a look of disappointment as she collected her package, shaking her head and walking off without saying thank you. Some people right.

I soon headed over to the barber shop after Uncle Matt came back and took over, seemed like a short distance, after all the barber shop was right across the street.

Danny boy, my old friend and personally my only friend, I'd go to the moon for this guy. I just hated those chairs though, always wondered why he couldn't get those regular chairs and used those instead.

At the barber shop, a guy was asking Danny if the new guy in town came over for a cleanup yet. "Not yet" said Danny with a smile as he winked at the fellow in the chair. Danny knows very well he'll be over sooner or later.

After the last customer was finished, Danny closed up the shop and asked me to help him bring out the chairs, four brand-new ones to be exact. Danny had already started to bring out the chairs and was asked for help with it, I already started to unscrew the old one's, but the rusty old screws gave me a run for the money. I hated those chairs.

Danny boy was always nice to me; he brought over a bottle of soda from the shop fridge and handed it to me.

"Hot day huh Trevor?" asked Danny smiling. I thanked him for the soda and replied "yes" but he could clearly see on my face that something was wrong. Old Danny boy knew me well, even when I try to hide my feelings. Growing up in this town, you come to appreciate certain things and one thing I appreciated was Danny, my first and only barber as a child growing up.

"Ok Trev" said Danny concerned. "What's up?"

It's evident; he called me Trev for short. Something he only does when we are in the social setting.

Danny boy was a good listener and friend, one you can always count on. In his late 60s Danny was like one of the youths, he had the ability to interact with any age group and foster friends from even the antisocial.

I don't know if it's the groovy earring in his right ear or just his hip talk that did it all.

After spilling the beans on my issue, it felt good getting words of encouragement and wisdom from Danny.

The one thing he said that stood out was the words, "all things made for you will be given to you, and if it's not for you then it's not yours". I couldn't thank him enough for always being a good friend, top with all the good advice he dispensed, but he just responded by saying "were even, thanks for setting up the chairs". We both laughed it up and said our farewells. I didn't know that it would be the last time I'd ever see Danny boy again. Still brings tears to my eyes.....

My street was pretty quiet at nights, except lately, the drilling, hammering and sawing coming from my dear neighbor's house across the street. Idiot couldn't have a time and place for nothing. I'd call Sheriff Hopper, but that would only make situations worst, making enemies with the new neighbor an all. A pillow over my head, and I'm out like a light.

Next morning the same hustle as usual to get out the house and off to work. Today I was in such a rush after getting up late, thanks to the noise caused by my inconsiderate neighbor, already ruined the day for me.

As soon as I opened the door, standing in front of me, face to face was the mystery man himself, my new neighbor.

The shock caused me to jump back, with a startled expression on my face. He said "sorry to startle you, I was going to knock, but you opened the door just before I could have gotten a chance do so" with a pleasant smile and a soft comforting voice. Man I said to myself, this guy was smooth. Anyway he introduced his self as Jeff Harding.

All I could come back to say was "that's ok" my efforts to introduce myself was met with an extended hand gesture for a handshake which I responded with a firm grip to matched with his strong grip. He went on saying how he tried on several occasions to come over but I'm never home or when I am home, he's busy working on the house. This was a strange event for me, this guy was actually nice and all I could come to say was "that's fine, I understand". He even apologized for the noise. Which all I could say was "what noise?"

"So I guess we will be seeing each other around and as soon as the place is finished, I really hope you could come over, so we could chill" he said with a smile. This was unbelievable for me but at the same time an allover great experience. This was the first person to invite me to their house to socialize and not to do something for them. I was actually flattered he wanted us to hang out.

We shook hands again as we both departed and went our separate ways, me off to the bus stop and him to his house.

The one thing I couldn't get out of my mind though was when I turned around for a brief moment. I caught this unusual look as he stood at his doorway, it was cold and

67

creepy one, and it was a look of pure and complete evil. It gave me a cold scary feeling.

At work the buzz was on the town dance and lime at the city hall, something held annually as sort of May celebration. It was good though, lots of food, drinks and laughs with friends and family. I was looking forwards to going this year with a date. By that I mean Ms. Alder I had in mind. What was notably about this year was the fact everyone who ask me about the dance, kept asking if I'm bringing a date this year and for me, it's something I've had in mind myself, sadly it isn't happening.
It started off very low on the radio but soon was raised louder by my uncle. It was the broadcast that changed my life forever.

On the news the top story today, the faceless killer struck again this time a family of four not too far from our town, as a matter and fact very close. The old mill road that was abandoned after foreclosure, it still had a few people living in that area. Those who grew up there refused to move after hardship met the area and the factory closed.

The report described that the owners of the hope town bed and breakfast and their two kids where found hacked to death in what investigators described as another faceless killer style killing. Which I may add, the faces of the victims were removed. The reporter when on warning residence in the area to be alert and vigilant at all times especially when travelling at nights.

The fact that this sort of serial killer was in our town caused some to panic while others just had a silent worried look on their faces as they stood silently listening to the broadcast.
Mummers and chatter continued, Hope town has never had a serial killer before and people here never had to worry about walking at nights because crime wasn't something frequent here at all, even murders here is so rare that, we haven't had one in years. Everyone knows each other and lived peacefully.

The air was one of depression and anxiety, with my uncle trying to assure the folks in the store that our sheriff will do his best to keep us safe and if that killer is in our town, he'll wish he never came here. My uncle said with great confidence as he turned to Jack Maubi and nodded his head.
Maubi was another general store owner but one who specializes in the sales of fire arms. "What of the dance?" a worried customer asked. "What of it?" Jack replied. "We will get security organized of course, I'll just talk to the sheriff and set up a patrol around the area" said Jack. "Well that sounds like a good idea" said the customer. "Of course it is" replied Jack giving the customer a pat on the shoulder and walking off in my uncle's direction.
Don't know what they were talking about but I was sure from the looks of it, it had to be about that broadcast and the serial killer, obviously.

The perfect start to my day, a serial killer in town and a possible cancelation of the town dance, it couldn't get worst until the thought crossed my mind. All this happened when my neighbor arrived in town. It couldn't be just a coincidence that as soon as he showed up, people got killed by a serial killer. This started to worry me a lot because I happen to be living right next to this weirdo.

This was something I had to let my uncle on, I wasn't sure how he would take it, but somehow I know he would be the best person to share my thoughts with, given the fact that all my crazy thoughts he somehow finds himself listening to and advising.

The time didn't come to talk to uncle Matt, so as I went over to talk to him, miss Gilbert, the neighbor that lives next to me, she had asked if I could come over later and help her put up some garden lanterns in her backyard. I normally don't have a problem with helping out around the neighborhood. It's something I've been doing for years now anyway. I figured the talk with uncle Matt could wait till later.

After dropping off the Donald's packages, I headed over to miss Gilbert's house. To my shock and surprise my new neighbor, Jeff was already in the yard helping miss Gilbert put up the garden lanterns, that AHOLE. Man that made me angry and nervous at the same time. The fact that this guy is trying to take away my neighborhood unpaid job and that he could actually be the Psycho at large.

Passing Miss Gilbert's place with my head turned straight and focused on my door, I heard Miss Gilbert call out to me. Leaning over the fence she indicated that it was getting late, and she didn't see me coming, so she decided to ask Jeff to help her out.

I raised my hand to her and said "it's ok". After which she returned to Jeff and the lanterns, the fun laughter I heard coming from her backyard, seemed to me like he is a funny weirdo, he raised his hand to me and all I could do is just smile, open my door and enter my lonely house. Closing the door I felt something I haven't felt in a really long time, it was the feeling of jealousy.

The next morning on my way to work, I saw Jeff helping his next door neighbor move out an old couch to his garage, That IDIOT. I used to do that, didn't really like doing it sometimes, but I did it anyway.

At the store Uncle Matt was in a meeting in his office upstairs. Seems like a meeting in relations to the town dance, because all the towns very important and senior people was there including the Mayor, town clerk and even the sheriff.
My Uncle Matt was sort of a senior man in the town, well respected, liked and most of all, a man who was reliable.

I went about doing my work as usual, when I noticed that Danny boy was missing in action but also with his work too, because I noticed from since yesterday the Barber shop wasn't opened for business, which was unlike Danny, I never saw him taking a day off or missing an important meeting, like ever.

Several calls when unanswered and persons in the area claim they haven't seen him around. I grew worried and uneasy. Telling Uncle Matt about the strange observation also made him worried too. He decided that we will check out the barber shop after we close up the store. Living upstairs in the Barber shop made things easy for Danny boy, he would get up early to clean up the shop before he opened and found it easy that way since he didn't have to travel too far to get to work.

The tension was building as we headed over to Danny's Barber shop. The cold feeling that something was wrong keep kicking me in the stomach.

The place was locked up tight, lights off, and strangely we could see from the shop window that his small hair bin was still in the corner of the shop not emptied. That's not like him, I thought to myself, something was definitely wrong.

Uncle Matt made a move to the door. He knocked several times, but got no answer. It wasn't a problem for Uncle Matt, an expert handyman always knows locks, which was no challenge for him and in a matter of seconds, the lock on the door was opened.

I remembered Uncle Matt saying, easy and breeze, as he looked up at me while still bent over in front of the lock.

I couldn't help noticing the uneasy look he had on his face, I guess we both were nervous, especially as we entered the barber shop, more so when a cold feeling hit us, like a gust of cold breeze rushing through the room. A strange feeling I'll never forget to this day.

On the floor was unopened letters that had blown off the table and was left lying on the floor, this indicated to me that Danny didn't come down in a while.

He was always neat and tidy and ran his business the same way, grooming was his business and cleanliness was his principle. He would never see something out of order and just leave it alone.

Uncle Matt called out for Danny several times but got no reply, the cold darkness of the barber shop surrounding us, giving us a bad feeling. We made our way up the stairway, which leads to down a corridor to the bedroom.

The door was slightly opened, and we could see dim light from the streetlight coming through the bedroom window and exiting through the open crack in the door. As we entered there was a foul smell that made me almost threw up, we could make out someone lying in the bed motionless. "Danny Boy" said Uncle Matt nervously. No answer. We drew closer to the bed and could now see that it was Danny lying in the bed.

Uncle Matt reached for the bedside lamp switch and switched it on.

"OOOOOH MY." Uncle Matt jumped back in horror as he covered his mouth.

I stood still as I stared in shock at Danny lying in a pool of blood with the skin on his face peeled completely off. I just couldn't move I was frozen with shock, staring at Danny's face; I came to notice his eyes were gone as well.

Furthermore, I could feel tears running down the side of my face and I still today don't know if it was fear, sadness or the horror of what I was looking at, a sight I would never ever want to see again or would ever forget, well I didn't get that wish.

"Cover him up with the sheet Trevor, I'll call the sheriff" said Uncle Matt. I stood in complete shock, I could barely move.

Uncle Matt tapped me on the shoulder and said "Hey, cover him up with the sheet". I quickly snapped out of the daze I was in and reached for the sheet. As I pulled up the sheet to cover over Danny, I could see the emptiness of his missing eyes staring at me. The sheet covering over his face now, I felt some ease in my mind enough to mutter the words softly, "farewell my friend".

70

Tears fell like rain afterwards but this time I know why. Uncle Matt pulled me away and hugged me, he knew how close we were, and it was evident to him that comfort was need.

"The sheriff is on his way, let's go downstairs" Uncle Matt said remorsefully.

Sitting outside on the barbershop stairs, a rush of memories came to me about Danny and the thought of how much I wanted to rip his killers face back off, these thoughts made me angrier than sad now. I started to ask myself what sort of animal could do something like that. Looking up at the streetlight with tears still in my eyes, my thoughts now on the faceless killer and who he could be, one thought came to me. JEFF !, it makes sense, since he showed up, the faceless killer struck here, and I was so sure he didn't even have an alibi.

Sharing my thoughts and suspicions with the sheriff and Uncle Matt led nowhere. The sheriff just said they will look into everything.

Lying on my bed was hard that night, I couldn't sleep, every time I closed my eyes, I could see Danny's eyeless and faceless corpse looking down at me, I would jump out my sleep terrified. I got up several times to get a drink of water as this often cool me down, when suddenly in the corner of my kitchen, I made out the shape of a man standing still in the dark corner next to the fridge, with blood running down his feet and spreading all over the floor. My kitchen lights were off, but light were coming through the window that cast a glare of light in the surrounding room.

I slowly moved over to the kitchen light switch, as I moved slowly I saw the head made a brisk movement and faced me, this caused me to jump back in shock, just then I switched on the kitchen lights. It was gone, nothing there, I sighed with a big smile. As I turning around briskly to go back to bed, I saw standing in front of me Danny's faceless corpse screaming RRRRRRUN! I JUMPED BACK IN TERROR falling to the floor covering my eyes. I started screaming out of fright.

Then suddenly I heard a knock on the door. I opened my eyes and the terrifying ghostly figure of Danny was gone.

I got up and went to answer the door, switching off the kitchen light, I cautiously looked around. As I opened the door standing in front of me with a concerned look on their face was Jeff. "I heard screaming and something falling down, so I decided to come over to see if you're ok" he said.

"I'm fine" I answered," just had a little accident that's all".

He turned his head slightly to look in and said "well if you ever need anything I'm just across the street" I said thank you and quickly closed my door.

Heading over to my easy chair, my mind was a rush with thoughts of confusion.

A so-called nice neighbor and my dead best friend, I couldn't help but notice how fast he came over to help out though, but most sociopaths are like that anyway and I still had my suspicions about him.

As I walked pass my bedroom window, I happened to glance out for a brief moment, across the street I saw Jeff staring right at my bedroom window with his curtains half pulled. As I stood there watching him, he stepped away from the window and pulled back the curtain. That sent chills down my spine, that night I didn't sleep a blink.

Hope Town news was a buzz about poor Danny boys murder, THE FACELESS KILLER STRUCK IN HOPE TOWN, the headlines read, looking at the news article, there was a picture of Danny boy on the front page in his happier days, a comforting face I'll never see again which has now been replaced with something that only had once existed in my nightmares.

"You can stop reading the articles now, we all are trying not to" said Ms. Alder. The shock of turning around and seeing her there caused me to pull down the paper in front of me so quick that it was now resting on my lap. "Hi" I said with a smile. "I just can't read that, I feel so sorry for poor Danny" she said while looking at the door. "Yea me too, he was my best friend" I said.

"I heard you and your uncle found him, it must have been terrible".

The sadness hit me hard when I think back as I said "yes".

My mood when all the way back up the highway when Ms. Alder said that Jeff invited her over for dinner at his house, and she'll be in my area this evening. I wanted to warn her and share my suspicions about Jeff but for some strange reason I didn't, I was thinking I shouldn't, and so I didn't.

All I could say was "good for you" and all "the best of luck". When Alder walked through the store door, everything in me was saying run up to her, grab her in your arms and kiss her, Tell her you're the right one for her and not Jeff, but I didn't, I just let her walk right out of my life forever. Lord knows if I had only known her faith I would have stopped her that day. I really would have.

That evening I could see from across the street Jeff's living room lights on, I know for sure he had company, because he never sits in his living room and I could hear the sounds of laughter coming from the room too, she never laughed with me like that, I thought to myself. It was 10 in the evening and the living room lights were still on. I made my was off to bed, pulled my covers up and went off to sleep, saying in my mind have a good time you A hole.

It was around 1 am when I heard a scream, I jumped out of my bed and headed to the window and looked out. The Hackson's who live next to Jeff had their lights on. They heard it too, so I wasn't dreaming it. Jeff's lights were off and he didn't turn it on for any reason. I saw Mr. Hackson looking through his window but gave up after seeing nothing. My mind ran over the situation as I started to think of Ms. Alder.

If he hurts her I said in my mind, I'll kill him and that would be the end of the faceless killer.

At the store, Uncle Matt was discussing the town dance Friday night and the security measures needed to be put in place, when all of the sudden a small boy burst into the store, Mr. Matt, Mr. Matt, the sheriff want to see you immediately, its Ms. Alder sir. "WHAT!" I shouted in shock. "Stay here Trevor" shouted Uncle Matt pointing at me as he raced out the store.

My mind was a mess, as I paced up and down. My thoughts running crazy, I didn't even notice customers coming in.

I waited for Uncle Matt to come back patiently. It was around 6 when he arrived. The look on his face told me everything, staring at me speechless and with those eyes of sadness, I know it was bad. He finally said to me "sorry buddy, I know….." he didn't finish because he could see the tears falling down my face. He said sorry again and turned and walked away. I stood there crying my eyes out looking up at the ceiling.

I finally mustered the bravery to visit the morgue the next day. I wanted to put closure to Ms. Alder's death and to confirm to my disbelieving mind that she was actually dead.

Looking at her lying on the embalming table brought back a rush of memories, even though we weren't very close, we did have a few good times together. I started to remember the first time I fell for her at the Hope Town Fair, her warm smile and kindness won my heart that night and ever since. I could feel the tears falling and soaking my shirt, Doctor Lance tapped me on the shoulders as he walked away in silence. Furthermore, I decided not to look at her face because I wanted to always remember her beauty the way I always liked it with the warm smile she always had on her pretty face which now gone because of a psycho.

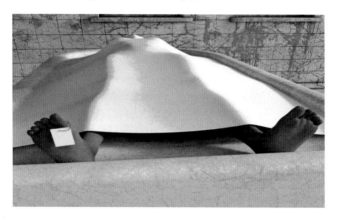

My tears of sadness soon turned into rage as I clinched my fits and bite into my lips so hard I could taste blood. JEFF was on my mind now, the faceless killer and revenge was the main dish I was going to serve.

I went over to my uncle's office, in a locked cabinet, which he and I carried the key for, was a 12 gage shot gun. I unlocked the cabinet and took it out, feeling the power of justice in my hands; I left the office carefully hiding the gun in a Duffel bag I use when I'm transporting large packages and headed over to my place early. Hiding the gun under my bed, I slowly got up while thinking to myself, why no one suspects Jeff? Next morning the headlines about the faceless killer on a rampage taking his second victim in Hope Town, had everyone inside and outside the store reading, I could literally see the fear in people's eyes as they read the article.

Some said "poor, poor Ms. Alder". I heard my uncle talking to a customer standing at the counter about Jeff being questioned about the incident but had an airtight alibi, since Ms. Alder was seen by her neighbor arriving home shortly after 1:30 am alone.

How did she end up in the middle street alleyway is the question and Jeff was home watching a horror movie around that time, the Hackson's confirmed hearing the TV loud and the movie was checked out with the time as well, Besides no one saw him leaving his house.

Jeff, I thought had everyone fooled, even Uncle Matt and the sheriff.

I decided to stay home the next day and call in for the day off, Uncle Matt was very supportive, saying take all the time I needed to recover, but I had other plans for the day. I was going to pay Jeff a little visit and do some investigating of my own. I wanted to gather all my evidence to be sure he was the psycho at large.

Furthermore, I waited for Jeff to leave the house and as soon as the coast was clear, I made my way over by Jeff's house. I snuck around the back to look for an easy way to get in, and I found one, a tiny window that led to the basement.

Uncle Matt showed me a trick how to pop those locks using a pocket knife and that's what I did, and surprisingly it worked very well. The basement window flew open in a second.

As I crawled through the window, I picked up the foul odor that smelled like something dead and rotting. I looked around the basement and saw a neatly organized basement, surprised this guy was very neat. Then I saw it, in the corner hidden away by a bunch of boxes. A couple of large trunks that looked vintage and very old. I recall these trunks when he first moved here as the trunks he was very defensive over when the driver asked if he wanted help moving them.

I slowly moved over to the trunks, from what I could see, it had old fashion locks, which I thought was no problem for me, nothing the pocket knife lock picker couldn't solve.

Moving the boxes away, I jumped back in horror. BLOOD! There were blood stains on the top of one of the trunks. "What the........" I said to myself.

I quickly pulled out my pocket knife and started fiddling around the lock with the knife, wasn't really sure what I was doing actually, just something I saw in the movies. When click the lock when and a latch flew out. It actually worked I thought to myself. Slowly opening the trunk, I almost threw up with what I saw inside. Chopped up body parts, a severed head well-preserved in a bottle, a bag full of jewelry belonging to females, one of which looked like something Ms. Alder wore and dead animals. "Jeff you sick FFFFF….." I said to myself.

Just then I heard a sound coming from upstairs, it sounded like walking. Shoot I thought to myself, Jeff must have come back home. He would kill me if he found me down here for sure. I quickly closed the trunk and tried my best to lock it back. Click the lock when as it locked back, I packed the boxes back on top of the trunks, thinking as I looked at four large trunks, more chopped up bodies, all victims of the faceless killer who now stood just above me.

As I turned and headed to the basement window, I saw something standing in the corner of the room covered in plastic. It looked like a mannequin. I moved over to take a closer look at it, barley seeing through the plastic, a shape and figure of a woman, my hand firmly clutching the plastic, I made a quick pull.

Standing in front of me was Ms. Alder with her hands stretched out. The skin on her face was gone but still recognizable as her and her eyes missing. She shouted at me "SAVE YOUR SELF" I jumped back tripping and falling with a loud crash into a bunch of well stacked boxes at the back of me. Falling to the ground, I felt a sharp pain in my side as I fell on something sharp that cut me.

Surgical scalpels, a box full of them. I could hear the footsteps quicken towards the basement door.

I got up and looked at the dummy mannequin standing in the corner and made haste to the window. Hearing the door unlocking, I made a desperate plunge through the window hitting the side of my rib against the concrete walkway outside the window. Getting up holding my side, I pushed back in the window and hurried off to my house.

As I stood at my door trying to quickly unlock it and enter, Miss Gilbert passed and was saying something to me about a birthday but I was in a hurry to go inside, I just waved her and said "ok bye".

I was sitting in my living room thinking about all that had happened, it made me fearful, sad, and excited about the fact I was right, I then got furious.

Picking up a flyer off my table for tomorrow's town dance I soon realized it was going to be a bloodbath. Everyone in one place with very small few homes alone. I closed my eyes and eased back in my chair and slowly went off to sleep.

A loud thump at the door woke me up, it was evening now. I slowly headed to the door but saw no one there, as I headed to my bedroom window, I could see Jeff's window curtains pulled and the shape of someone standing watching me from behind the curtain. I started thinking, did he know I was in his house or did he suspect me? A feeling of fear came over me as trying to sleep that night was very difficult, the images of what I saw in the trunk hunted me. I was prepared to bring in the Calvary tomorrow and put this to an end once and for all.

The next day, trying to tell Uncle Matt what I saw in Jeff's trunks was overpowered with the fact that I broke in his house and unlawfully trespassed.

Uncle Matt was upset and looked at my claims as over reacting. He said if he told the sheriff about this and they go over and find nothing which he said he was sure was the case, I could get charged for breaking and entering.

I found it ironic that I was sent home to take more rest. He did make a point though, my eyes were sleepy from lack of sleep and my nerves were shot from all the pressure I was experiencing lately.

I arrived home late that evening. I took a walk in the Hope Town Park to ease my mind a little. I noticed when I arrived, my neighbors as well as most persons in the street wasn't home. Probability at the town dance I thought.

As soon as I got in my house and locked up, I heard a knock on the door. I opened the door and standing in front of me was Jeff.

"Hey I just noticed you got in and I said to myself let me come over and take up that invite I promised you" he said with a smile. "I hope you don't have any plans for this evening because I put a lot of work into planning this evening invite for you" he said anxiously.

I thought to myself as I stood and stared at him.

He took my best friend, my neighborhood, my love and my peace of mind and nobody would do anything about it, and now he wants to lure me to my death. Enough was enough.

"Sure Jeff I'll be over in a few, just let me get my coat" I finally answered with a patronizing smile on my face.

I when over to the closet and got a trench coat that I had gotten some years ago but only wore once. I when into my bedroom and got the shotgun from under the bed which was well hid in my trench coat.

I slowly walked over to Jeff's house and noticed the lights were off. Sure preparing for me and the lights in the house was off. Jeff opened the door and silently moved away. I saw him heading into the dining room.

"Do come in Trevor, I've been waiting for you" he said in an unusually deep tone. As I entered the dark house, Jeff made no attempts to switch on the lights, it slowly dawned on me what was going on, alone in the house of a psycho. "What's with the darkness, did you forget to pay your electric bill?" I said sarcastically.

"No Trevor, the darkness is meant for you" he said in a low deep tone as he moved around the dining table, the light coming through the curtains helped me to pick up some of his movements very easily. I reached in to my coat with my right hand and gripped the gun tightly. "Is that so?" I asked.
"Why yes, I have a surprise for you" he replied as he moved around the table, I could see a carving knife in his hand gleaming from the reflected light shining on it. He walked out of the dining room and moved towards the living room door way with the knife clutched in his hand. I backed up a little and found myself bracing the front door. I felt a feeling of terror coming over me as my hands was shaking and beads of sweat ran down my face.
The thoughts of my life and the life of the ones he took from me rushed in, a trill of adrenaline, hope and courage. Looking at the knife that could seal my faith in Jeff's hand and feeling the gun in my coat, gave me the option to stand frozen in fear or fight for life.

There comes a time when a man must be a man, even if no one believes him or would fight for him and for me that day was today. A time to stand up and fight when you know you are right.

"Oh yea Jeff, I got a surprise for you too" I said with a burst of confidence.

As he moved closer and now stood in the living room, he replied "Is that so, well what it is?" No sooner had he completed his sentience, than I quickly pulled out the shot gun, aimed it right at his head and pulled the trigger. BANG! The shot gun pellets scattered hitting Jeff's face, I could see blood splatters all over the living room walls. Jeff's body fell to the floor with a loud crash, his motionless body told me he was dead, with a pool of blood now spreading out all over the floor. Jeff the faceless killer, was dead.

"In your face, faceless killer" I said laughingly.
Just then, I heard screams coming from all around the living room. I was very confused and shocked.
The lights went on, and Uncle Matt was standing at the light switch, my neighbors and the sheriff rose up from behind the couch and other living room furniture wearing party hats.
In the living room I could see a large birthday cake on a table and above a streamer that read "HAPPY BIRTHDAY TO OUR #1 NEIGHBOUR TEVOR". Now covered with blood spatters along with the birthday cake on the dining table.

In all the confusion that was going on in my life, it slipped my mind my birthday was today. Ms. Gilbert tried to tell me the other day but I was so taken up with what was going on I didn't pay attention. I was looking around the room at all the shocked faces staring at me speechless. Looking down at Jeff's faceless dead body, I slowly realized I made a big mistake.
He was trying to bring over the carving knife for my birthday cake. He and everybody had planned a surprise party for me. Dropping the gun to the floor, it was only a

matter of time before the sheriff arrested me. Uncle Matt just stood in disbelief at what I did and didn't say word.

At the courthouse, the prosecutor really did a number on me. Even though Uncle Matt got me the best lawyer, who even tried the insanity defense, the evidence didn't look good in my favor.

Jeff Harding, special effects and movie props expert. He was working on a movie production for some corny horror flick called Tears in the Dark. The body parts found in the trunk was movie props and the jewelry was special effects was well, the dead animals were preserved animals that just wasn't preserved well causing the bad smell and the blood, that was fake too. He was a private guy, loved by many and respected by all, and I killed him.

The prosecutor went hard on me, pointing out jealousy and the breaking and entering as proof of my delinquency. He even tried to point out that I may just as well been responsible for the faceless killers victims since I was jealous about Jeff and his relationship with Ms. Alder and the fact I commented a lot about Jeff's free haircut from Danny Boys barbershop.

This idiot prosecutor thought of everything, he literally nailed my ass to the wall. Guilty was the verdict and seventy to life was the sentence. There was a lot of time to think about life now; I spent most of my time looking out my cell window.

In all the confusion looking around the living room that evening, I could recognize most if not all persons their but one, a stranger was in that room.

There was someone I couldn't make out and the only person looking at me and the body not shocked or surprised but delighted somehow, as a matter and fact happy. I thought to myself, could this be the faceless killer, but I just left it alone. I was wrong before and because of it I finally got the vacation I so needed.

The dangers of an over thinking mind haunts me as I turned and stared at the iron bar door, I could see the horrid faceless figures of Danny Boy, Ms. Alder and Jeff standing in the cell side by side. They were saying "don't worry; we are going to be here for you, now and forever". Their crooked mangled smiles from their faceless figures caused me to scream in terror.

As they walked towards me, I don't know if I'm laughing, crying out loud or still screaming.

A young city police officer returns to her hometown only to be greeted by a haunting mystery about the town she grew up in and thought she knew. She will have to come to grips with reality as her faith is put to the ultimate test.

Arriving home after many years seemed a bit different for Lisa Bell, especially when she left at age twelve and moved to the city to live with her aunt and uncle. The warm welcome she received from her mother on the Bell farm comforted her troubled mind as she entered the house. Looking around she could see nothing has changed, same old house just the way she left it and remembered it.

The living room still had the old three-piece set, wall divider and armor. The mahogany china cabinet with all its components packed neatly, it seemed untouched for years. Looking at the stairway, now displayed family pictures which decorated the side wall all the way up to the top of the stairs. The dust on the window's barley allowed light to enter them, but the old curtains didn't do it any justice either, tick and dusty.

"I see the place hasn't changed much mom" said Lisa with her suitcase clutched in her hands.

She turned to look at her mother who was now walking towards her after closing the front door. "Well yes dear, don't get many visitors and your dad is retired now". "He spends most of his time in the barn with Paul our farm hand".

Betty Bell a stay at home housewife and mother of three, she was very much involved in the life of her family just as much as the running of farm with her husband Gary Bell who was now a retired City Hall Senior Councilor.

"Have you been in town yet?" Betty asked. "No not yet, just wanted to come home and rest up first mom" Lisa replied while putting down her suitcase.

Just then, her father came in through the back door and greeted her with a hug. It was the warmest show of attention Lisa ever remembered.

Her father was always serious with them, once she remembered a show of affection when he said "take care and always be safe" however, that was when she was leaving with her aunt and uncle to head to the city. So this greeting caught her off guarded and by surprise.

"I'm glad your home sweetheart" he said as he picked up her suitcase. "My you have certainly grown" he smiled "nothing like what I saw in those picture and video calls". He turned to face Betty, who looked at him with a smile. "Well yes dad I'm not here to stay, I'm on administrative leave" Lisa said with a half-smile. "Right, you're a big city cop now" he replied proudly while looking at Betty one more time. He turned with the suitcase and headed up the stairs. "I hope you remember your old room?" He asked, as he turned around halfway up the stairs.

"Yes I do dad" Lisa replied with a smile.

78

Making her way to the room brought back old memories of childhood, especially running up and down the stairs with her brother and sister and playing hide-and-seek. Her brother always liked to slide down the stair rails and she remembered she did it once, this always made her dad angry but it was fun anyway. This made her miss her siblings, especially when she hasn't heard from them in years.

Unpacking her things in her room made her think a lot about Crag, her partner who mysteriously when missing while investigating one of the most troubling cases they ever encountered. This sent her into a state of sadness, after all, they have been partners for many years and to her, Crag was a close and personal friend.

A knock on the door and Betty entered with a pleasant smile.

"How is the room dear?" Lisa turned around with a quick smile. "Same way mom, nothing has changed since I left" Lisa turned and faced the open window. She could feel a cool breeze coming through the window that was blowing up the curtains. She had almost forgotten how cool and breezy it was home compared to the city.

"Well when you're settled in, iv laid out supper on the table for you downstairs" Betty said with a warm comforting voice.

"Thanks mom, I will" Lisa said with a smile as Betty exited the room and closed the door.

Lisa dropped herself in a sitting position on her bed while holding a picture of her and Crag at the policeman's ball. It was taken when they first started working as partners. Staring again at the window with the picture in her hand, tears fell from her eyes.

Supper was like old times, her father reading newspapers at the table and her mother busy as a bee doing something in the kitchen with the occasional visit at her chair and one spoon of supper, and then she was off again. "So how are things in the city?" Gary asked while reading the newspaper.

"Like the city dad, hard work every day and less time for yourself" Lisa said while putting a spoon of her favorite dish into her mouth. She loved apple pie as a child and would often as her mother to make it. It was something she rarely made, only on special occasions. Her mother really went out of her way to make everything right for her homecoming and with baked custard on the way for dessert. She was sure what breakfast and lunch would be like tomorrow.

"Betty told me you got an award of some sort" Gary said while folding the paper in half and resting it down at the side of the table. "Yes it was for a case me and my partner was working on". "Oh so it's true you are a supper cop" he said smiling. Lisa with a bashful look on her face replied "I wouldn't say so dad". "How is Crag by the way?" He asked looking at her puzzled as to why she didn't mention anything about him.

Crag was the name often mentioned in phone conversations, one time her father made a joke by saying "when will we meet our son-in-law".

It was a joke that often made Lisa blush. "I'm not sure dad" replied Lisa looking down sadly.

Her father noted the sadness in her face and decided it best not to pry but move on and change the subject. "Ok, so did you go into town yet?" He asked cheerfully. His expression relaxed her a bit as her father didn't regularly smile and moving off the topic brought some relief. "Not yet but that's one thing on my list to do" she replied with a smile. "Speaking of which, where is Paul, Corn Grove king of the corn" she asked with a big smile that soon turned into a little chuckle.

Gary got up briskly and headed to the kitchen phone, completely ignoring Lisa's question.

She could see from the expression on his face when asked about Paul that this was one of those leave it alone things and decided to returning the favor he gave her earlier and moved off the subject, finishing up supper, she got up from the table and headed to the kitchen sink.

The house and yard looked so much the same as she could remember as a child, staring out the kitchen window reminded her of the good times as children. They had attached a rope fitted with an old tractor tire to a branch on the tree house to make a swing. They enjoyed taking turns pushing each other on the swing. She was surprised it was still in the backyard attached to the branch and the old tree house remained the same.

The warm feeling of long almost forgotten memories of joy came over her as she remembered her brother and sister playing hide-and-seek in the barn house and playing catch running like crazy all around the yard.

These memories soon faded away when she remembered her mother rushing into her room in a crazy haste to packing her things, without a minute's explanation, she was rushed out her room and into her aunt and uncles waiting car. Her mother standing in the doorway uttered the words "I love you Lisa" very softly as the car drove off. That was the last they ever spent time together as a family.

Lisa took a comfortable seat on the porch swing that faced the front gate, it was always a place of comfort for her as a child, she would remember sitting with her mother talking and when it was storytelling time with her sister, her brother would always be the silly one to creep up silently behind the swing to jump scare them, but it was fun she remembered.

"Hello Ms. Lisa" said a tiny soft voice.

Lisa quickly snapped out of her flashback daydreaming mood and turned to the front gate.

To her surprise, a pretty little girl sitting on a little red bicycle, she had red ribbons in her red hair and a white dress with red flowers. What Lisa thought was the cutest thing she ever saw since she arrived home.

"Hello there" Lisa replied with a smile. Getting up from the porch swing, she headed down the stairs and towards the gate. "And how do you know my name may I ask?" she asked politely with a pleasant smile.

"Your momma said you'd be coming home, I sometimes pick up things from the store for her, and she always gives me sweet snacks" she said with a full set of grinning teeth. "Oh that's nice, so what's your name?" Lisa asked. "It's Mary Louise Tomkins" she replied once again with a full set of grinning teeth. "Well hello Mary Louise, how old are you"? "I'm seven and still growing" she replied. Her reply made Lisa laugh.

They were soon interrupted by Betty, who came out the front door shouting the words "Mary Tomkins, why are you so late?" Lisa looked down at the bike handle and noticed a plastic shopping bag marked Steve's groceries. "Sorry miss Betty, there was a line at the store today" she said with a smile. Betty came down the front stairs with a tray of chocolate chip cookies. "Oh don't fret dear" she said while lowering the tray of cookies. Mary wasted no time to grab a few and shove them into her little red bag. Betty also handed her some money which she took and put into her pocket. After saying thank you in a polite manner, she handed the groceries to Lisa and said goodbye. Lisa replied the same to her as she rode off and said "see you again soon Mary Louise".

She waved them off as she rode away, and they waved back. Betty asked Lisa if she cared to take some cookies, picking up one from the tray, Lisa said "could I ever say no to that". They both laughed as they headed inside the house.

The next day, Lisa decided to take a trip to town. Gary pulled the old Chrysler out the garage and parked it in front of the gate. "I think this is more suited to your style" he said while wiping the hook down with a cheese cloth. Lisa smiled and said "Dad you know I'm a common girl, a style for me is a spoiling for others" they both laughed as Gary handed over the keys.

"Be safe sweetheart" he said. Lisa jumped into the driver seat and started the engine, she turned and replied "I'm a big city cop remember, don't worry" they both laughed as Gary gave the old truck a tap on the side. Lisa waved him goodbye as she drove off.

Her first stop was a place that brought back memories she shared with her school friends, their favorite hangout spot.

Linda's Dinner; the dinner was famous for its special ice cream sundaes, four layers of various flavors of ice cream and chocolate syrup topped with sprinkles and a cherry. It was popular especially among the children in town, but it was also loved by the adults who had no pride to order up one. Second to that was the large gum drop candies that stood on the dinner countertop in a large glass Mason jar, Lisa remembered coming home from school in the afternoons with her friends and stopping in at the dinner just for one of the gum drops, they were big enough to provide the required sugar and sweet satisfaction they were looking for and one always did the trick. It only cost a penny, but it was always worth the treat. She remembered bothering her mother some mornings before she went off to school for the extra penny just so she didn't miss out on the sweet treat.

Standing at the doorway was a wash of memories and how much the dinner haven't changed at all, even the curtains hanging on the windows were the same design, she could see as she entered the door, the gum drop jar was still in the same place and the famous ice cream sundae was still being advertised on the menu board.

A small price increase shocked her as this would make Linda's Dinner sundaes famous, not only for its contents but for the cheap price.

Looking around, she could see the same old diner tables and chairs and the smell of Kenny's bacon being cooked on the grill, bacon and eggs was always her father's favorite when he came, and he would always order it as his usual.

"Well hello Lisa" said Linda smiling as she looked up and saw her, she was wiping the counter top and talking to old papa, he was called the towns lumber jack because he worked up at Ben's Logging's, some towns folk would say with the years he's been working their he should have owned the place by now.

"Come on over here girl" said Linda with a smile, "It's good to see you gal" she said gesturing her hands in a calling fashion. Linda now a single middle-aged business-woman after years of searching finally decided on making the business her only love and the passion she drives into it shows in the prosperity of the establishment.

"Come over here and let me fix you up a sundae". Lisa wasn't going to refuse that offer, walking up to the counter. She took a seat right next to old papa.

Old papa smiled at her as she sat next to him, an old crooked smile on a face of a seventy two year old man who she had known from childhood, he used to always

81

scare her and her friends as children because he was tall, serious and scary looking. To her now he was just a quiet and peaceful old man drinking his coffee.

As Linda served up the sundae to Lisa, she said "it was on the house" Lisa thanked her and said "if this is the welcome hospitality you get, then I'll come home more often" they both laughed as Linda said "I'm glad your home". "I'm glad to be home" replied Linda with a pleasant smile.

"What is this world coming to these days?" Linda asked looking at the daily newspaper lying on the counter.

The headlines read "The faceless killer strikes again killing a family of four, "it's really sad, a family of four this time, horrible" Linda said disgusted, dropping the newspaper she asked "How do you manage with the city girl?" "I manage" replied Lisa while taking a spoon of sundae into her mouth.

The sheriff entered the dinner standing at the door looking around, fitted with a dark shades over his eyes and a wide smile on his face, especially when he saw Lisa, he started walking over to where she was sitting. Leaning his elbow down on the counter next to her he said with a smile "Isn't this a pretty picture".

"Good day sheriff Tony" she said while taking another spoon of sundae and turning away her face. "I didn't know you were in town, or I would have taken you around" he said with a grin.

"Thanks Sheriff, but I can make my way around" she said while putting her spoon into her half finish sundae, she got up from the stool and thank Linda, she then said farewell to Sheriff Tony and left. She could her him saying something to her as she was walking to the door, but she was too anxious to leave and didn't want to turn around to ask what it was he had said or cared to do so either.

Driving around town, Lisa noticed how everything remained strangely the same, for some strange reason nothing has really changed.

It was like the town was frozen in time.

Returning home, Mary Louise was on the front porch playing snakes and ladders, "You know, it's much more fun when you play against someone else" Lisa said as she walked up the front steps.

"I don't have anybody else to play with, just me miss Lisa" she replied with a sad expression. "Well today you will challenge me" Lisa said with a smile as she sat next to her. Mary's eyes lighted up with excitement, she quickly reset the game and took out the extra token from the bag. As they started to play, Mary knew she was very good at the game, but Lisa had coped a four win over her three making her the victor when Gary pulled up in the driveway.

Mary indicated it was time for her to go home before it gets late, her mother gets paranoid when it gets late. As she got up from the porch chair, she hugged Lisa, something that caught her by surprise. "Thank you for playing with me today, I had a lot of fun" she said while still hugging Lisa. "That's ok Mary, you can come over, and we can play anytime" Lisa said as Mary ended the hug and picked up her bag.

As she was leaving, she turned and said "you're like the big sister I never had". This melted Lisa's heart as she waved her goodbye. "I see you made a new friend" said Gary with a smile. "Yes and a few more in town too, the unwelcome kind that is" she replied. "Yea I know I ran into Sheriff Tony today" Gary said while handing her one of the shopping bags, it had a heavy package inside marked Hope Town Dairy produce. "Mind helping out the old man" he said, "Anytime dad" Lisa replied taking the shopping bag and heading inside.

The next day, Mary Louise came over early in the morning, Betty was surprised because she's never over that early, she asked for Lisa as she entered the living room, she took a seat in one of the chairs and dropped her bag down on the carpet.
Lisa was surprised at her early morning visitor, "Well this is an early surprise" she said as she walked up from behind. Mary turned around and said "hi" she pulled out a gum drop candy from her pocket and offered it to her.
"I know you like gum drops" she said with a wide smile. Lisa took the candy and thanked her as she put it into her pocket.
"I have somewhere to take you" Mary said while getting up from the chair and picking up her bag. "Ok cool" Lisa said, "I'll get prepared, and we can go".

Mary and Lisa walked into the woods taking the back route over the farm fence, it was a place she was never as a child allowed to go, and her parents never told her why. They crossed the old windmill and milling house, it used to be the main wheat provider for the community until the city business owners came with their wheat stocks.
Continuing on up the back trail passed the mill, was an oddly abandoned cottage and well not too far from it, seems like no one has lived there for ages and Lisa never heard of an old well in the area before.
All the way on the journey Mary and Lisa talked, she kept asking her questions about the city, if she had kids, if she was married and what being a police girl was like.
Lisa was amused by her questions while some made her laugh, Mary held her hand all the way and sometimes pulled at her to show her a retreating rabbit or a squirrel running up a tree.
They finally arrived at a clearing in the woods, at the far side she could see a small lake and a tall tree, next to it was a smaller tree and on top was a small tree house. Mary pulled her hand to take her to see the tree house. It had a rope ladder leading all the way up to the top. "Made it myself you know" she said with pride pointing at the tree house.
"That's great dear, but I don't know if I really should" Lisa replied while looking up nervously.

"Come on it will be great, plus its safe, I come up here all the time" she said while tugging at Lisa's hand. "Well if you insist". Lisa said while putting her hand over her face with a nervous smile.

She followed Mary all the up to the top of the tree house and entered through a small cut out in the center. It was small inside with three windows. There were a lot of books packed neatly in the corner of the window that faced the lake. The tree house was well covered with big branches flourished with many leaves. It provided good shade and a cool environment.
"This is a really nice tree house Mary, you did a great job" Lisa gave her a thumbs up.
"Thank you" she replied.
"My dad showed me what to do and how to cut the pieces and I did the rest" she said. It was peaceful and relaxing up in the tree house Lisa thought. She lay back on a

mattress stretched out on the floor and rested her head on her forearm. The rest of the day, they talked about a lot of things, moving from one topic to the next.

It was getting late as the sun was going down and they both lost track of time, Lisa couldn't help noticing how anxious she was to leave as if she was afraid of the dark, but it was indeed a long way back, and she didn't walk with a flashlight either, getting caught in the dark would not be a good idea.

As it was late, Lisa offered to take her home and she would find her way back, Mary didn't mind since it wasn't far from the tree house. As they arrived at Mary's home, she could see an anxious mother waiting on the porch, she turned to Lisa and hugged her "goodbye Lisa, Thank you for coming today" she said.

"Thank you for taking me, I really had fun, the most I've had in a long time too" she said as Mary turned and headed through the gate. She waved her mother who waved back with a smile.

It was almost dark when she started to head back. It was a good idea to take her home first she thought. Cutting through the trail passed the old cottage it was dark, she suddenly got a strange feeling, a feeling like she was being watched.

Looking at the cottage she could feel eyes watching her from inside, the torn and worn out curtains blew up with the strong breeze as she passed it.

The sounds of old creaky hinges from the doors inside could be heard and a strange eerie sound that came from inside that sounded like someone was inside whispering. She quickly hastened her steps and soon arrived back home.

The next day, she was off to visit an old school friend, Rebecca was her best friend, they shared a lot of good memories together, a memory she would always remember and never forget, was the time, when Zed Carter use to bully her in school. Rebecca would stand up to him for her. She always represented her against other bullies as well. Arriving at her home surprised her. She was married with three children now. "How did you find me?" She asked with a surprised look.

"I'm a cop you know" they both laughed and hugged as Rebecca invited her inside. She was introduced to her husband and children then invited to sit in the guest room where they could do some catching up. She served Lisa some sandwiches and a cup of fresh brew tea. They spent hours talking about old times and trying to catch up with what was going on in each other's lives. "So no hussy or kids yet, huh?" Rebecca asked. "No not yet" Lisa replied while putting down her cup of tea.

"Your dad told me something about someone you were seeing at the academy?" She asked. "Yea that was long time ago" she replied with sad expression.

Rebecca moved on after she saw how uncomfortable the question made her, "so I bet you haven't been keeping up, Louie Parks and Diana Housings, as in glamour girl Diana, disappeared right after you moved". Rebecca said while picking up her cup of tea and taking a sip. "Really?" said Lisa shocked. Louie Parks always liked her in school, he would offer to carry her books and help her with homework. "Yep, they were never seen again". "Guess you left at the right time too". "Why is that?" asked Lisa. "A string of strange disappearances started taking place after, children around the same age too. It first started in the countryside then the town. We were kept home from school until it suddenly stopped". Rebecca said while putting down her cup of tea.

The strange story shocked Lisa, she was speechless and now more questions crowded her mind about her strange movements away from home as a child.

They moved off-topic and started to talk about other things as well as cracked a few laughs. Rebecca was very good at jokes, she used to be the life of the group and the funny one. Lisa remembered one time when they were children just before school closed for summer vacation, they spent the last day at the dinner telling jokes and having fun. Rebecca told so much jokes, Lisa remembered laughing so much her jaw and sides hurt.

As Lisa said her fair well to Rebecca, she told her to "take good care of her family and herself". Rebecca returned the same wishes as she made one more joke. "Remember to look me up when it's the wedding" Lisa laughed and said "I would never forget". They hugged and said their goodbyes as Lisa left.

On the drive home, her mind kept coming cross the strange story Rebecca told her, as she approached the driveway, she saw Sheriff Tony and a Deputy standing outside the yard next to the gate. Sheriff Tony was talking her father and a deputy was talking to her mother. Sitting on the porch was Mary's mother crying uncontrollably.

Lisa exited the truck and walked over to her mother who was closest to the gate as s h e entered. "Oh, thank goodness your home honey" Betty said as she hugged Lisa. "What's going on mom?" asked Lisa. "It's Mary Louise, she's gone" replied Betty. "Gone" shouted Lisa shocked. "Yes on her way over, she never arrived, we searched town and the nearby village, but she can't be found anywhere, she never did this before". The sheriff and Gary soon walked over to Lisa. The Sheriff told them that he will do all he can to find her, and they will keep searching. The deputy walked over to Miss Tomkins and escorted her to the patrol car, he said "don't worry we will get you home". She replied "I want my daughter home, that's what I want", she then turned back and walked up to Gary and said angrily "This is your fault, all your fault, you promised us this won't happen again". The deputy pulled her away and said "it isn't anybody's fault, we will find her" he escorted her back to the patrol car.

The sheriff said good day folks then drove off followed by the deputy. All the events was too much for Lisa to take in at once, she tried to keep her composure while at the same time process the information. As they entered the house, Betty told Lisa to go upstairs and get some rest. The shaken and sad Betty Bell walked off to the kitchen as though she was in a daze. Gary sat in his regular easy chair, staring up at the ceiling as though he was lost in thought. Lisa went up to her room silently with a troubled mind, as she sat on her bed staring at the window, she could feel the tears running down her face. There was a strange feeling in her stomach she hadn't felt in a long time but quickly linked it to the news of her missing partner.

Her memories of Mary clouded her mind, especially her cute smile and pleasant voice. For the second time in her life, she lost a close friend and there was nothing she could have done to stop it.

Pounding her fist into the bed angrily then wiping her tears from her eyes, she got up and headed over to her writing desk. Stashed under it was a bag she thought she wouldn't have the need to use in a hurry. Pulling it out from under the desk and opening it, she could see shinning in the sunlight coming through the window, her badge.

She picked it up and held it close to her chest, "I will not lose you too Mary".

Lisa picked up her cell phone and called the station in the city, "Can I speak to Captain Quagmire?" asked Lisa. Quagmire now promoted to captain and in charge of Lisa's division. "This is a surprise" said Quagmire. "Remember you owed me a favor, well I'm cashing it in now" said Lisa, "you're not the type to take up a favor unless it's really important, so what do you need?" asked Quagmire. "I require a clearance to work a case in my hometown and access to the police encrypted database" said Lisa. "Ok it will take some doing, but I'll call the chief, he can get on to someone from the Marshals' office that should be able to set that up, and I'll text you the login information to the database". "Thanks captain, we're now even" said Lisa as she hung up the phone.

After the conversation with Quagmire, Lisa headed over to Mary's tree house to start searching for clues.

Betty tried to talk her out of taking the case, she said "the police here will take care of it, they always do". Lisa kissed her on the forehead and told her "thanks for always protecting me but it's time I found out the truth".

Passing the detectives exams and turning down the promotion, didn't make her less fit to handle a case as this. Her partner always had her back but this time she was on her own.

Searching through Mary's things in the tree house, she came across a strange drawing of a person in a hooded coat but nothing else out of the ordinary. Her next stop was at the town police station, she was greeted with smiles from sheriff Tony who leaned over his desk pushing his face close to Lisa's face, she moved away and walked towards the window in his office as he sat back in his armchair and said "I'm glad that you're taking the bold move to help out, but this is a state matter in which we the local authorities will handle" he said coldly.

"Appreciate that sheriff, but you will see that clearance was given from the Marshals' office for this district, instructing full cooperation with me". "Yes I did see the memo on your temporary deputizing" he said once again coldly.

"Thank you sheriff, I will be requiring access to case files on the disappearances that took place thirteen years ago and Oh I will also need witness statements taken on this case" sheriff Tony sat back in his chair with his face crossed and flushed with anger. "Will there be anything else Marshal Lisa" he asked in a sarcastic tone. "Not at the moment, I'll be downstairs waiting on the archives keys" replied Lisa in a sharp professional tone as she walked out the office and closed the door.

The deputy she saw at her home assisted her into the archives and handed her the keys, he was very polite and offered to help if she required. Lisa however told him she was fine and continued to gather the records of disappearances from the shelves.

The files where in four boxes, she combed through each file, searching through witness testimonies and statements, fourteen children missing and not a trace, no clues was left by the kidnapper or kidnappers and no motive.

She did find one thing strange while searching, all the missing children were abducted eight days apart respectively, she wasn't sure if this was actually a clue or just a coincidence or the kidnapper planned his or her time for the abductions. The last victim they found a bracelet and her bicycle at the corner of the road where she was abducted, but there was something else too. Lisa couldn't make it out from the crime scene photo. Taking out her notebook, she noted it down to check into. She also noticed that things were missing from the evidence box as well. The bracelet they found was gone. It was late when she had finished up. It was going on to seven she noticed from her watch and the feeling of tiredness was stepping in. She packed up neatly all the files she had laid out on the evidence room table and exited the room. As she's heading out the station, she saw the deputy again who this time identified himself as deputy Crag, she stared at him with great surprise.

He asked if something was wrong, but she told him his name reminded her of someone she knew a long time ago. There was an awkward silence as they stared at each other. She then broke the silence by asking if he could provide her with any information about the last victim who disappeared.

He asked "anything specific?" Lisa replied "yes, her bike had something suspicious on it, like a chemical substance". He said "yes we know, it was embalming fluid, homemade formula used during the early 17th century, it let off a strange glow due to the Strontium and other chemicals mixed".

She thanked him for being such a big help, once again there was an awkward silence before they smiled and said goodnight.

The strange chemical and the days were still lingering on Lisa's mind as she walked through the parking lot fiddling with her car keys. Suddenly, she was stopped by something strange that ran past her. As she looked around only to she saw a small child standing in the dark empty parking lot opposite her. "Hey, you startled me, what are you doing out so late?" Lisa asked smiling but couldn't see the child's face as then stood motionless in the dark parking lot. "She hurts us" whispered the child. "What did you say?" asked Lisa in shock. Just then the child fell to the floor.

Lisa rushed over and started crying out for help, she picked up the child in her arms and said "everything is going to be ok" as she reached for her cell phone, the light caught a glimpse of the child held in her arms, it was the skeletal remains of a child. She immediately dropped the remains in shock, causing her phone to fall also. She backed away slowly starting at the dead remains that was before her. She could feel her heart racing and her mind wondering what's going on. Furthermore, she soon mustered up the courage to slowly walk over to her phone and retrieve it while turning on her phone flashlight, she slowly walked over to where the body was. To her surprise, the body was gone and a child's school bag was left.

The name Keith Smith was written at the top of the bag, she recognized the name as one of the missing children. Looking around she couldn't see anyone around, she picked up the bag and headed to her truck.

In her room, she began searching through the bag, everything in the bag was normal school accessories, except for a drawing book which contained strange writings that looked like ruin symbols, as she turned the pages, a drawing stood out, one similar to the drawing she saw in Mary's tree house with a name at the bottom, Lady of the Meadows.

This baffled Lisa, but it was a name she heard before, a game children use to play. Her memory of the game came back and how it went. **Run! Run! Run! From the Lady o f the Meadows, whose woes no one knows, pray she don't cut off your toes, say a prayer you better care and beware the Lady of the Meadows.** She always hated that rhyme but it couldn't be by just chance it popped up and something worth checking into.

The next day, Lisa was checking the police database on her town, she was shocked to find an old missing persons' case since the 1950s. Lisa read the article; a child went missing near the old well in Corn Grove on Monday 9th June 1952. The police questioned the child's father Paul Paxby who last saw the child before he left for school.

"Wait, Paul Paxby is our old Paul. I never knew he had a son". This revelation settled on her mind as she headed to the garage to talk to her father.

Gary was busy servicing up his car engine but when Lisa questioned him about Paul's missing son, he stopped what he was doing and immediately took a seat on a stool next to the corner of the garage.

He told her it's time she heard something he and her mother was keeping from them all these years. Lisa quickly grabbed a stool from the other end of the garage and sat next to him.

Lisa listened attentively as Gary spoke and didn't interrupt not for a second, he was very nervous at first but after taking a deep breath he began talking.

"Our fore parents, Paul and a few other folks around here were the first settlers here in Corn Grove, back in those days folks were very religious and upheld strong morals. There was one who came with the early settlers, a woman and a child, Medea Schumer was her name, and sadly she had lost her husband to a strange illness. She was only looking for a new start and was welcomed by all but there was something else, it was discovered with her child first, complaints from her classmates maintained that she was drawing symbols that looked witchcraft in nature.

A town council meeting was held, and the mother was brought before the towns e l d e r s with the child. It was then discovered that there strange beliefs were indeed so to be witchcraft in nature or so was the thinking back then. They were both trailed for witchcraft and were found guilty. It wasn't in the nature of the council to harm them but to reason with them in an attempt to convert and save them but other folks had other ideas, in fear that witchcraft power would bring down the town. A band of villagers forcibly one night took both of them from the prison and led them back to their home, the old cottage house on the far side of the woods. There they took j u s t i c e in their hands, locking both of them in the cottage and setting it ablaze. They could hear her screaming the words from inside the burning cottage "I WILL COME BACK FOR YOU AND YOUR GENERATION". The next day the villagers found her charred remains, but the child was burnt completely to ashes". As he finished the story, he looked at her with a sad expression and said "I'm sorry Lisa. I couldn't tell you our family secret".

Lisa was speechless, she couldn't even move, after several attempts to get up from the stool, accompanied by several uneasy turns and swivels. She finally did and walked slowly and silently towards the garage door.

After a moment of silence between the two of them, she finally spoke "So you are saying that a ghost is taking revenge on people of Corn Grove because of something our fore parents did decades ago?" He lowered his head and said "the strange disappearances that have been taking place for generations, yes sweetheart, when it started back we rushed you away from here because we saw a pattern".

"What pattern?" Lisa asked curiously

"Some generations boys are taken and the next girls". He continued "every eight day for eight months it happens, she returns to take children".

Lisa did notice the pattern though with some inconsistencies on the gender, the age did look familiar, and it made some sense that a timeline for the abductions was set in stone. However, something didn't add up, a ghost doesn't leave prints.

Lisa told her father she would continue her investigation until she uncovers the truth and find Mary. She told her father what their fore parents did is not our fault, and he was still the greatest dad in the world.
He tried to caution her as he revealed to her that Paul when missing a few months ago investigating a lead he said he got. He didn't give many details, but he was excited about the lead as he was convinced it would solve the case, he never stopped s e a r c h i n g for his son.
It was the one thing that ate away at him for many years and as a result, Paul never lived a happy life ever since.
She promised him that she would be careful as dangerous work is something she was accustomed to and cases such as these often turn out to be nothing more than a ghost story.
As they hugged, Lisa could remember a very few occasions when they actually hugged and that was when she was leaving home as a child. She had fewer memories of her father's affection, but it was taken in with much appreciation since she came back home. She was glad all the missed years were finally being made up between them.

Going back to her room, she fired up her laptop and started searching the police database again for anything she could find, checking child abductions with similar patterns and any leads on the cases.

Finally, she came across something similar, but she wasn't sure if it meant anything, she read a report from five years ago, New Brooksville a countryside village in Corn Grove recorded three strange disappearances of children between the ages of eight and twelve years old.

The town ranger Rango Allan gave a statement to state police that investigations were on the way and full cooperation and assistance is coming from the Corn Grove sheriff's department.
Lisa eased back on her pillows and rested her head on the bed rails, from the report she saw the timeline of disappearance was eight days apart, same as the cases in Corn Grove.
She started pondering on the name Rango Allen, a name for sure she was going to check out.

The local sheriff's department in Corn Grove is in charge of the entire district but because of limited resources and personnel, a ranger is often appointed by the sheriff's department to oversee law enforcement in the small villages. The work set out for the rangers are similar to that of the local police, and they have a greater responsibility of maintaining law and order in the area.
Lisa realized that time was running out, if indeed all the rumors about the strange disappearance was true, then in eight days another possible kidnapping might take place and the possibility of ever finding Mary Louise might be lost.
Getting up from her bed and closing her laptop, she headed over to her writing desk and picked up her truck keys, she settled in her mind that the journey to New Broomsville will be a very long and tiring but one that had to be taken.

Arriving at the ranger station in New Broomsville, Lisa recall only visiting the countryside twice on trips with her father, she had forgotten how beautiful it was and how fresh the air was there, the breeze blows heavily with clear fields that go for miles.

Ranger Rango came out to meet her with the most unwelcoming expression, as though he was really unhappy to see her.

As Lisa questioned him about the disappearances and his investigations into them, she slowly realized that he was not going to be helpful at all.

Saying goodbye to Rango felt like a disappointment to her as he apologized to her for the wasted trip, but something caught her eye when he came up to the truck to wish her a safe journey.

It was a charm bracelet one worn by females, she found it amusing and very unusual that he would be wearing one, but that wasn't a cause for suspicion.

It was dark when she got back home. Parking the truck in the garage and heading around the front porch she was suddenly stopped by something moving in the corn fields.

As she continued looking, a small child came out carrying a basket. "What are you doing out so late?" Lisa asked walking over to where the child was standing.

As the child stepped into the light that was coming from the porch, Lisa could see clearly that it was a girl about eight years of age and of native decent. The child's face looked pale and hands feeble as though she was malnourished, when she looked up at Lisa, she could see the sadness and suffering in her eyes. "Oh my goodness, what happened to you?" asked Lisa in shock. The child took something out the basket and handed it to her.

Lisa noticed a charm bracelet on her wrist, one similar to the one she saw on Ranger Rango earlier. She collected what looked like a parcel wrapped in brown paper, the child said "beware the Lady of the Meadows, she now seeks you" after the child finish speaking she turned and walked back into the corn field and vanished.

Lisa couldn't believe what she just saw, holding the package in her hands and staring into the dark Corn fields, all her life of reasoning and believing that the supernatural was just superstition has now been change.

Clearing her head and looking down at the package she said to herself "She can have me but not Mary".

Back in her room she examined the parcel. She could see the parcel was old from the age of the paper. Opening it she found a nurses uniform inside, holding it up she saw a small rectangular badge with the name Lydia Schumer, Lasco General Hospital. This hospital was located in the city, and she could tell from the age of the uniform that it was early vintage 1900s. The nurse's uniforms were changed decades ago including the badges worn.

Putting down the uniform, Lisa picked up her laptop and stated researching the title Schumer.

She found a few persons with the title from all over the world but one from Windsor City by the name Cira Lee Schumer. Clicking on her social media page, Lisa found something very unusual, a photo of her and a group of friends standing next to an old building with ruin symbols.

Her mind went all the way back to the first clue left at the station in the bag of the missing child.

Quickly going to her writing desk, she pulled out the bag stashed under it and took out the drawing book.

She began researching the symbols inscribed on the pages, and strangely the symbols meant stepping stones. This baffled Lisa as she continued to check the ones in Cira's picture. The meaning of the symbols shocked Lisa, the eight-ball clan. "What the….." said Lisa in total shock.

The case started to get even stranger now with all the bits of clues that seem to add up and others that didn't, but there was still something that baffled Lisa still and that was why Ranger Rango was so reluctant to help her?. Researching Rango went nowhere. There was nothing on him not even a social media account. However, checking the police database, Lisa hit the jackpot, a file from the office of professional responsibilities investigating the use of unnecessary lethal force by officer Rango Allan district 13 Windsor City police.

Reading the file, Lisa uncovered a closed case involving the shooting to death of two unarmed suspects by Rango some eight years ago, he was terminated from the police force but a no case submission was submitted by the D. A's office.

It all started to make sense now. The Allan's from research were successful business people who excelled in the manufacturing of popular pharmaceutical products. Rango Allan, the youngest son of the Allan's seemed to have been running with the wrong type of company at an early age, from DUI s to drug bust at a house of users but outside the police encrypted database there was nothing on the records. It seemed to her that his records was sponged away to cover for him.

Checking his appointment record for Corn Grove, she found that sheriff Tony was the signatory and not the council. "Very interesting" said Lisa rubbing her chin.

It was almost midnight when she wrapped up her research and she was very tired, turning off her computer and returning it to the writing desk. She suddenly got a strange feeling, the feeling like she was being watched.

Switching off the desk lamp and now standing in the partial darkness of the room, she slowly walks over to the bedroom window and looked out. To her shock and surprise, she could see the silhouette shapes of hooded persons in the surrounding fields, it was dark, but she could make out the outlines clearly, suddenly, she saw one standing right below her window in clear view.

She was able to see the figure clearly because of the side light, she saw crooked pale hands pulling down the hood to reveal the burnt face of a woman in her mid-thirties, one of her eyes was completely burnt out and part of her hair was burnt off. Lisa gasped in horror as she saw an evil terrifying smile.

Lisa stood and watched as she pulled the hood back over her head and walked towards the trail where she and Mary had taken to the tree house. The others also went back into the field then vanishing into the cold dark woods.

That night Lisa couldn't sleep at all, despite how tired she felt. The memory of the face she saw still stayed on her mind and the words the child told her, that the Lady of the Meadow was coming for her next.

Lisa was out of her room and on the hunt again, this time checking the part of the field she saw the Lady of the Meadow vanished. She wasted no time for the usual early morning breakfast and didn't take the normal chat time with Betty.

She checked the trail and found traces of the same embalming substance found on the victim's bike. Not only that, but she continued searching more up the trail and found something interesting. A fresh gum wrapper, and residues of the contents still fresh on the wrapper. Lisa knew that someone was on the trail recently.
Heading to the old well, she got a cold uneasy feel as she approached it.
Looking down the well, she could see that the water had dried up years ago, but there was something else, at the bottom of the well.

Lisa pulled out a tiny flashlight from her pocket and shined it down the well, shocked in disbelief, she saw a fresh shoe print coming out from the walls of the well. Lisa's mind started calculating all the clues as she shouted "Bingo!"
Running back to the house as fast as she could, she headed up to her room and picked up her cell phone. She called deputy Crag at the station and told him what she thinks she found.
She told him to make contact with state police. He agreed that he would call everyone he could immediately and come over as well.
After hanging up the phone, she went over to the writing desk and pulled out her bag. She took out a service revolver from her bag and loading it, she held the revolver up in front of her and said "it's you and me now miss Lady of the Meadow".
She quickly put the gun back in the holster and secured it on her waist, with in a flash, she was out the door briskly heading back to the trail.

Walking up to the old cottage, Lisa put fear out her mind and entered, nothing looked disturbed as she looked around but as she walked around searching, her feet stepped on something. A hollow sound came from a newly made part of the floor, strange she thought as she bent down and dusted it off. A lock that secured a trap door below was discovered, she looked around for a blunt object and finding an iron bar she used it to break the lock and open the trap door.
She saw a dark stairway leading all the way down. Pulling out her flashlight she switched it on and started to walk down the dark stairs.

She could smell the scent of dead rotting flesh as she came to the bottom of the stairs, shining the flashlight around she saw symbols and writings on carved out walls.
An old wooden table stood at the corner of the room with a small opening that had some light coming through it. Lisa walked over to were the light was coming from only to find a small wooden door.
It had a vintage lock and a symbol on it. She used her police training to kick down the door and entered.
Lisa couldn't believe her eyes. In the small room, she was surrounded by what appeared to be a torture chamber, from chopping blocks, to operating tables with surgical equipment and some medieval methods of torture devices. In the far corner she saw a small cell with bars, someone was in there. She quickly ran over to it and found Mary Louise lying on the floor. "Oh my goodness, oh my…." said Lisa shocked and excited.
"Mary, Mary" she cried, but there was no reply. She looked around the room and saw a metal cabinet, heading over to it, she saw it wasn't locked, when she opened the

cabinet she saw file folders. Her only interest was to look for the keys to the cell. Tumbling through the shelves and knocking down the folders she saw something interesting falling out from one of the files.

It was a file on Cira and among them where others too, she saw something shining in the dim light, it was the keys.

She quickly snatched them and headed to the cell. Unlocking the cell and entering, she could see poor Mary passed out on the floor.

Holding her up in her arms she stroked the hair from her face while calling her name several times nervously. She slowly opened her eyes and spoke with a soft weak voice "Miss Lisa…. I know you would have found me". Lisa hugged her tightly laughing with delight. She could feel tears of joy coming down her face. "Let's get out of here" she said smiling. Picking her up from the floor, Mary's feet was too weak to walk, so she carried her in her arms. She could see another beam of light coming through a crack in the wall, it seems like another trap door was down there and a possible was out.

Suddenly, she heard a noise from the outside, shining her flashlight at the stairway, Rango appeared holding a machete. "You little ….." he said angrily. He started running towards them holding up the machete high above his head. Before he could get close to land a blow, Lisa picked up a small stool next to the table and flung it at him, knocking him down to the floor.

She could see him struggling to get up off the ground but realized that the way she entered wasn't going to be her way out anymore.

She headed to where she saw the beam of light in an attempt to see if she could find a way out through it.

Pulling away at some thin plaster that covered it, she saw drawings on a wooden door, ones that looked like a child's drawings. Pulling open the unlocked door, she saw a dark passage way. Shining her flashlight down the passage way, she saw light coming from the end. "There must be a way out there, let's go" she said to Mary while lifting her up in her arms. She started running down the dark and narrow passage.

Looking back, she could see Rango on his feet again coming towards them. She continued quickly ran down the narrow passage way until saw a small crawl space. She quickly pushed Mary through and then following, she could hear running footsteps behind her coming closer. To her shock and surprise, she was in the well, switching off her flashlight, she saw something shocking on the walls. The walls had a glowing substance with the same ruin symbols from the drawing book that translated steeping stones. She could see that the stones on the wall with those words were loose and could be used to climb up and out the well.

Lisa helped Mary up as she told her to keep climbing just like the tree house and don't look down. Just then, Rango pushed his hand through the crawl space grabbing Lisa's leg.

Mary started screaming as Lisa is pulled to the ground in a struggle to free herself from Rango's grip. "Keep going Mary, keep going" cried Lisa as she kept fighting to free herself. One strong kick to Rango's face, and she was free.

Quickly getting up off the ground, she started to climb up the well. She could see when she looked down, that Rango was now through the crawl space and was trying to climb up after them. Grabbing Lisa by the foot again, she could slowly feel her self-loosing grip.

Suddenly, the well started filling up with water, as Rango looked down and said "What the……." Pale crooked hands of children came out of the water grabbing him by the leg and pulling him down.
Lisa could see the many faces of the missing children now dead surfacing as they pulled the struggling Rango down to the bottom of the well.
Lisa wasted no time but to hurry and climb out of the well. Looking down in the well she could see the body of Rango floating on the water. Picking up Mary in her arms, she started running away from the well. As they ran through the wood they were suddenly stopped by dozens of hooded figures who appeared from behind the trees and surrounded them. Lisa pulled out her revolver and aimed it at them. "Stay away" she yelled. The figures stood motionlessly, as she turned to look for a way out but soon realized that they were surrounded.

Then suddenly, coming out from a clump of trees, the Lady of the Meadows could be seen floating in the air heading towards them. Her terrifying screams and grotesque face struck terror in Lisa's heart as she fell to her knees hugging Mary tight in her arms. Looking up at Maida who was now in front of her suspended in the air, she screamed out loud "You can have me anytime, but you're not going to take her" Lisa held up the revolver and fired three shots at Maida, she heard a cry of pain as the Lady of the Meadows fell to the ground motionless. The other figures that s u r r o u n d e d them slowly moved back behind the trees and vanished.

Lisa hugged Mary and told her to stay put as she went over to investigate. Holding her revolver in front of her, she pointed it at the motionless body of Maida. She walked up slowly and cautiously while constantly looking around to make sure the coast was clear. Standing over Maida, Lisa cautiously kneeled down then pulled up the hood that covered her face.

She could see blood coming from her nose and mouth and the cold stare of death in her eyes, on her hands she felt a familiar substance, it was make up, her face looking up close appeared to be a stiff fitted rubber mask. Lisa peeled away a lifted piece she noticed sticking out at one end to reveal the face of Cira Lee Schumer. On her waist was a safety line attached to an overhead motor powered pulley system that became broken when she fell and embalming substance on her hands to give it the appearance of a dead person.

Standing to her feet, Lisa turned to Mary standing in the distance and said with a smile "Let's go home".
As they approached the farm house, she could see the state police, the sheriff's department patrols and the state marshals, patrol cars where everywhere. "Remind me to thank Crag when all this is over" the both laughed as they walked towards the gate. Police and emergency teams rushed them, putting blankets around them and escorting them to an ambulance.

An old familiar face came up to her, captain Quagmire accompanied by the head of the state marshal's office. "I had to come myself when I head you needed help" Quagmire said with a wide smile. "Thanks captain" replied Lisa looking up at him with a smile. "So what really went down here?" asked the head of the state marshal's office.
Lisa explained, "Maida Schumer did die in the fire decades ago but not her daughter, she taught her to escape should anything happen through a crawl space that leads to the old well, she marked steeping stones in ruins only visible when you're looking at it from the bottom as it was written under the steeping stones, the symbols of course, she taught her daughter to read. This of course could be used in the event of an emergency. It was the same knowledge that ironically condemned her in the first place.
She eventually grew up and became a nurse who worked at Lasco General Hospital by the name Lydia Schumer. She got married later on and had children in which Cira Lee Schumer was a descendant and head of a murderous cult called the eight-ball clan. Cira decided to keep her mother's title and went by the Schumer title. This title fueled her obsession of her grandmother's curse and the local urban legend held by the people of Corn Grove. She quickly turned this obsession into beliefs in witchcraft that soon turned violent and very deadly.
They started first sacrificing and killing animals but soon worked their way up to small children, Ranger Rango met Cira in the city and probably was one of the wrong crew he was running with before his removal from the police force. He was one of the key members of the clan and he protected Cira as they moved here years ago to avoid suspicions after investigations to the same patterns of disappearances started up in the city, I found some files in the cottage which were police reports taken from the city police records on Cira and another one containing a report filed against her for stalking children in New Brooksville, all of which Ranger Rango covered up.
They decided on concocting the urban legend after her great-grandmother's legacy down to the costumes and props something Cira was good at as an acting major at the city university.
"Well done officer or should I say detective, I guess when you get back" said the head marshal as she turned glancing at captain Quagmire with a wink.
She then stuck out hand to shake Lisa's hand. As she was walking away, she turned around and said "You know if you ever want a change of scenery, there's always an opening at the marshals' office for you" "No I think she's just fine in my department" said captain Quagmire. They all had a good laugh.

Quagmire tapped her on the shoulder "see you whenever you get back detective" he smiled as he walked away.

As she got up from the ambulance, Sheriff Tony walked up to her, he extended his hand to shake hers as he said "Well done officer" but Lisa kept her hands folded in the blanket.

"You know I found it strange that Ranger Rango knew I was investigating a hunch near the old cottage, and he was actually in town and not at the ranger station" she said while looking at Tony with a suspicious look. Sheriff Tony's face went serious, the smile now gone and replaced with a pale expression of worry.

"My investigation is far from over Sheriff Tony" Lisa said in a serious tone with her face flushed with anger as she slowly walked up to him, they stood face to face as their eyes locked in a serious stare.

"Far from it" she said biting her teeth as she brushed pass him jamming his shoulder, he stood motionless as she walked away.

In the house, Lisa could see the happy embraces from family and friends surrounding Mary Louise, her mother came up to her and hugged her. Her father said proudly "that's my big city cop daughter" as her mother said "well this calls for a celebration, cookies and coco for everyone". Everybody laughed as some said "finally". It was happiness all around.

Mary broke away from her friends and family when she saw Lisa and ran towards her, with tears of joy in her eyes she hugged her. Lisa hugged her back and whispered softly in her ear.

"You're safe now".

The End
****

DEAR READER

The author of this book would like to thank you the dear reader for taking the time to share in this journey. It is readers like you who preserve the essence of great literature, because, in reading you open up a world of learning and adventure, where you can explore new and wonderful things. It is with great hope you enjoyed this book and found satisfaction in reading and if so, please do look out for **Tears in the dark** part 2 coming very soon.

The second series of this book will offer much more pictures and stories as the mystery and suspense intensifies, will we ever know who the faceless killer is? Will we ever catch him? Or, whatever happened to Arthur and Crag?

All this and more in part 2, so keep reading and exploring and never stop learning.

Best wishes

Shawn Freeman

Made in the USA
Columbia, SC
04 May 2023

16053470R00055